The Young
HUGUENOTS

D0917351

THE HUGUENOT CROSS

AND ITS MEANING

1. A variant of the Maltese cross was the basis of an insignia awarded by the French kings to soldiers and statesmen.

2. The Huguenots (French Protestants) claimed the symbol (with slight variation) as Frenchmen and as "soldiers of Christ."

3. The eight points of the cross came to symbolize the Beatitudes [Matthew 5:1 - 12] — marks of the true people of God.

4. The crown of thorns symbolizes the Huguenots' identification with Christ in all their persecutions and martyrdoms.

5. The four heart-shapes between the crown of thorns and the centre of the cross depict the hearts of God's people centred upon Christ alone.

6. The dove speaks of the Holy Spirit, the strength and comfort of God's elect in their pilgrimage to the glory everlasting.

Alan C. Clifford

Huguenot Inheritance Series # 4

The Young HUGUENOTS

by

Edith S. Floyer

INHERITANCE PUBLICATIONS
NEERLANDIA, ALBERTA, CANADA
PELLA, IOWA, U.S.A.

Canadian Cataloguing in Publication Data
Floyer, Edith S.
  The young Huguenots

  (Huguenot inheritance series ; 4)
  ISBN 0-921100-65-5

  1. Huguenots—France—Juvenile fiction. I. Title. II. Series.
PZ7.F652Yo 1998   j823'.8   C98-910869-4

Library of Congress Cataloging-in-Publication Data
Floyer, Edith S.
  The Young Huguenots / by Edith S. Floyer.
    p. cm. — (Huguenot inheritance series ; #4)
  Summary: In 1686 in France, after their parents and older brother are
killed by the soldiers of King Louis XIV, four young Huguenots decide to
flee to Amsterdam and embark on the dangerous journey.
  ISBN 0-921100-65-5 (pbk.)
  1. Huguenots—France—Juvenile Fiction. [1. Huguenots—France—
Fiction. 2. France—History—Louis XIV, 1643-1715—Fiction.
3. Orphans—Fiction.]
  I. Title. II. Series.
  PZ7.F672Yo 1998
  [Fic]—dc21   98-42051
                                                             CIP
                                                              AC

Quotations of the Huguenot Psalms are from the *Book of Praise: Anglo-
Genevan Psalter.*

With thanks to the Reverend Doctor Alan C. Clifford of Norwich Reformed
Church (Great Britain) for lending us an early edition of this book.

Second Printing 2003

All rights reserved © 1998, 2003, by Inheritance Publications
Box 154, Neerlandia, Alberta Canada T0G 1R0
Tel. (780) 674 3949
Web site: http://www.telusplanet.net/public/inhpubl/webip/ip.htm
E-Mail inhpubl@telusplanet.net

Published simultaneously in U.S.A. by Inheritance Publications
Box 366, Pella, Iowa 50219

Available in Australia from Inheritance Publications
Box 1122, Kelmscott, W.A. 6111 Tel. & Fax (09) 390 4940

Printed in Canada

Contents

When speaking about the Huguenots, one often hears the exclamation, "I am also a descendant of the Huguenots!" Considering the fact that thousands of Huguenots were dispersed over the whole world, especially to Canada, England, The Netherlands, Switzerland, South Africa, and the U.S.A., it is very likely that 30% of the North American population has some Huguenot blood running through their veins. Of the Protestants it may well be the majority that has some connection with those who were martyred and exiled for their faith. Eight generations back our forefathers number approximately 132. One of these ancestors may very well have been a Huguenot. But, aside from the family connection, all descendants of the Reformation, who maintain the Faith of the fathers, will realize the kinship we have with these brothers and sisters in Christ. This kinship, and the example of their faith, has moved the publisher of this book to launch a series of books entitled:

HUGUENOT INHERITANCE SERIES

# 1 - *The Escape*	by A. Van der Jagt
# 2 - *The Secret Mission*	by A. Van der Jagt
# 3 - *How They Kept The Faith*	by Grace Raymond
# 4 - *The Young Huguenots*	by Edith S. Floyer
# 5 - *Driven into Exile*	by Charlotte Maria Tucker (A.L.O.E.)
# 6 - *The Refugees (a Tale of two Continents)*	by A. Conal Doyle [2004]
# 7 - *Done and Dared in Old France*	by Deborah Alcock (published)

Most titles in this series (except for # 1 & # 2) were published for the first time about one hundred years ago. It is our prayer that these books will be read by many people in thankful remembrance of those who were faithful unto death, for the glory of God, and as encouragement to live also in faithfulness and gratitude before our Heavenly Father.

Roelof & Theresa Janssen

All the books in the Huguenot Inheritance Series are independent stories written by different authors.

I

At St. Croix

"I do not care what you say, Henri, it is very disagreeable, it is not at all fair, that we should be treated as babies, and that Aurèle should know everything."

The speaker was a girl of fourteen years old, who paused at the bottom of the see-saw, keeping her brother in the air, that she might give utterance to the above sentiments. She was a very pretty girl, and the scene around her was also very pretty.

It was a rambling sort of place, half garden, half plantation; fallen trees and long, rank grass mingled with brilliant flowers which flourished in wild luxuriance. It was surrounded on all sides by a wood, principally of fir-trees, but toward the west an opening among them showed a pretty chateau at a little distance, and beyond that, far away on the horizon, a line of purple hills, behind which the sun would soon go down.

Marie de St. Croix was the only daughter belonging to the chateau; a brilliant, dark-eyed little maiden with long, dark hair, a rosebud of a mouth, and roses on her cheeks. Three of her brothers were with her; Henri, her twin-brother; Guillaume, little more than a year younger; and little Louis, a lovely child of five, who was almost as much petted as his sister Marie. He was sitting on the grass making a daisy chain; Guillaume was suspended in the air at the other end of the plank, patiently waiting till Marie should choose to release him; Henri, who was taller and rather fairer than his sister; with bright brown hair, hazel eyes, and clearly-cut features, was standing thoughtfully beside her, leaning against a pile of old moss-grown logs. After a little pause, he spoke in answer to Marie, "Aurèle is older than we are, you know."

"Bah! It is not two short years. Were we not fourteen last week!" exclaimed his sister, leaping off the plank with a suddenness which sent Guillaume flying on to the grass near to Louis, where he settled himself comfortably without any remark, or even a look at his sister. She, taking as little heed of the matter as he did, walked impatiently away among the shrubs, still speaking to Henri, who followed her as a matter of course.

"Not two years," she repeated; "and to be sixteen is not to be so very old after all. Henri," and the great dark eyes that she turned on him suddenly flashed with tears, "you know it is not that I am jealous of Aurèle, not that I do not know how brave, and noble, and love-worthy he is; but oh, Henri, I want to be brave and noble too! I know why it is, since that dreadfully sad Sunday when we had no service in the church, and all the people were crying, that they have all those secrets, that Mamma and Papa and Aurèle go every week and spend nearly the whole night away. I guess what they are doing. Do not you?"

"Perhaps," said Henri, soberly.

"Confess it then, do you not want to go also, instead of being hushed out of the way and sent to bed with the babies? Are you not also ready to die for your religion?" and the little maiden's face glowed and her tone grew almost fierce.

"I wish to go — yes," answered her brother, in the same quiet tone. "But I sometimes think — Listen, Marie," he added, suddenly lifting up his head, so that the western light shone upon it and showed a look in the deep brown eyes which was not often there. "We have talked of such things all our lives; we have been always waiting for the danger, and how has it been? We have lived here happy and safe all our lives; we have never had even to be secret till now. Marie, I remember this, and it makes me think — what if we could not do it? How can we tell what we would do and dare? I cannot take in the idea of anything different from all our lives. Can you?"

But Marie had not been attending to the latter part of his speech, or it is doubtful whether even her devoted love for her twin-brother would have saved Henri from a burst of indignation and contempt. She was straining her eyes to make out two figures who could be seen, through the opening in the woods, drawing near to the castle. Almost before Henri had finished speaking she exclaimed, "It is the father, and Aurèle with him. Let us come on to see him, Henri; it is so long since he has been to the castle in the day." And both children broke into a run.

Meanwhile Aurèle de St. Croix and his companion had already reached the castle, and were passing down a rarely-used passage which led from a small side door to the salon. The father, as Marie had called him, was now in truth a Huguenot minister; but, unlike most of his class, he had retained a dress which differed but little from that of a Romish priest, and still loved to be called by a title which Huguenot pastors did not generally claim. He had many reasons for so doing; and as he lived in too retired a part of the country to hold much communication with his Reformed brethren he had escaped all strictures on his conduct. He was now getting old, and his hair was already white; yet at sixty-three his figure was as upright and his eye as full of life as were those of Aurèle de St. Croix, the fair, handsome boy who now entered before him into the salon, saying, "Here is Father Gabriel, dear mother."

Madame de St. Croix, a slight, graceful woman, with a strong likeness to her daughter Marie, broke off in the midst of a sentence to her husband, and hurried forward as Aurèle spoke.

"O Father Gabriel! We are in such trouble. One does not know what to think — how to decide. For myself, I am ready to stay here, to brave everything, but he thinks differently. Tell him, my Louis."

"We were agreed before; is it not so, Gabriel?" said Monsieur de St. Croix, holding out his hand with a grave, sad smile to the curé. "Little wife, do not grieve so; it must have come to this sooner or later."

"Have you had fresh news then?" asked the curé, drawing his chair to the table with the air of one who was perfectly at home.

Madame de St. Croix had sunk into a low seat, and leaned against Aurèle, who supported her with a sweet, boyish dignity. Monsieur de St. Croix stood drawn up to his full height, regarding them with a look that would have seemed stern to those who did not know him. It was he who spoke in answer to Father Gabriel, "Yes; there is no doubt that these dragonnades are to commence in our neighbourhood without loss of time. And there is but one course left — a speedy flight."

"Should you attempt to leave the country?" asked Father Gabriel, thoughtfully. Both he and his cousin De St. Croix had been too well prepared by a long train of circumstances for this determination to waste words in regretting it.

"Not if I can help it," answered Monsieur de St. Croix, knitting his dark brows. "It may be only a temporary flight after all;

remember that, little wife. I propose to make first for St. Louis-de-Linard, and remain there for a while, till it is certain whether or not his Majesty will proceed in his godly work to the end. If it be a thunderstorm — though I fear it has already gone on too long for that — why, you may see us again, Cousin Gabriel, before the year is over. If not," and the brave voice took a deeper tone, "God only knows; but I trust He will enable us to escape to England."

"Ah!" exclaimed his wife, with an involuntary cry; "Father Gabriel, is it quite impossible that we remain here till we know whether or not we must go to England? To leave our home, our poor people. Louis, you are not afraid that we should yield; why, then, should we not wait here?"

"Because," said her husband, very quietly, "sooner than you should be exposed to such atrocities as have taken place at Nîmes, at Angoulême, no, at Périgueux, scarce a league from here, and that not two days ago, I would run my own sword into your heart."

Madame de St. Croix cowered in her chair with an irrepressible gasp of terror.

Aurèle, who had not yet spoken, bent down over her to whisper, "Courage, sweet mother; God is in the storm — He will surely see us safe through it."

"When do you propose to start?" asked Father Gabriel.

"As soon as it grows dark," said Monsieur de St. Croix. "Most of my preparations are already made; but there are the children, little wife."

"Yes, Louis; I will go and see that all is right. Aurèle, will you call them in. They should rest first."

"Yes, Mother." And Aurèle opened the door for his mother to pass out, but lingered for a moment himself to listen to what his father and uncle were saying.

Gabriel de St. Croix had risen, and the two were standing side by side upon the fireless hearth. Monsieur de St. Croix was in reality only ten years younger than his cousin, but few who looked at them together would have guessed that they had been friends and companions almost all their lives. Louis had the same tall, soldierly figure and keen, dark eyes; but his black hair had only lately become streaked with gray, and there was an air of vigorous determination about him which was altogether different from the grave, resolute bearing of the pastor.

But that there was a rare, deep love and sympathy between these two men no one could doubt who had seen the gesture with which Louis de St. Croix put his hand on Gabriel's shoulder as Madame de St. Croix left the room.

"You will not come with us then, Gabriel, *mon ami?* Your mind is quite made up?"

"Quite," answered Gabriel, quietly. "It is as clearly my duty to stay as it is yours to go. My people and I have lived, and we will die together — if it come to that. God grant that we may not be found wanting!"

"It is goodbye, then," said Louis, as the cousins clasped hands. "I feel like a coward," he added with a passionate emotion which Aurèle had never seen his father show before; "and yet I know that it is right. O Gabriel, my friend, my friend!"

"It is *au revoir* also," answered Gabriel, with the grave, sweet dignity in which, boy as he was, Aurèle already resembled him. "God bless you, dear Louis, and keep you under the shadow of the eternal wings."

There was an instant's silence in the room, and then the two Frenchmen drew closer together for a moment, and kissed each other for the last time.

Aurèle, feeling that he could remain no longer an unobserved spectator, slipped quietly away, and went to find his sister and brothers. Henri and Marie came running up the terrace as Aurèle came out upon it.

"Aurèle," cried Marie, "has Father Gabriel come? We saw him with you just now."

"Yes; he is in the salon with Papa," answered Aurèle, taking his sister's hand. "But you must not go in there just now; they are busy, and Mamma wants you."

12

"O Aurèle, is it more mysteries?" asked the girl wistfully. "Tell us, dear Aurèle. What does it all mean? We are not children, Henri and I, and we will be so brave!"

"That is right, Dear," said Aurèle, who felt that they must be told something, at any rate. "Then you will not cry and make a fuss if I tell you what we are going to do. We are going to leave home for a while, because Father does not think it safe here just now, and we are going to the chateau at St. Louis-de-Linard."

"But, Aurèle — going away?" asked the bewildered child. "When are we to go? And why is it not safe? Nobody has hurt us yet because we are Protestants."

"No; because it was not against the law till last year. I can't stop to make you understand just now, Marie, because Mamma is waiting for you; we are going to start tonight. Go to her; she asked me to fetch you all. I suppose Louis and Guillaume are in the wood?"

"Yes. But, Aurèle — tonight? Oh, poor Mamma!" added Marie, with a quivering voice.

Henri had not spoken a word. And now he only took Marie's arm and led her into the house while Aurèle turned toward the plantation from which they had just come.

He went straight to their usual playground and as he came out upon the half-cleared space, a last ray of sunlight straggling through the opening showed him a pretty picture against the dark background of firs. It shone full upon the long golden curls and white dress of little Louis, who still sat with his hat off and his lap full of daisies, close by a pile of logs, which were half covered with the trailing leaves and delicate white blossoms of the bindweed. A tangle of cabbage-roses were dropping brilliant petals on the long grass in which lay Guillaume dreamily relating a story in a low, monotonous tone, almost like a chant.

Louis saw his brother directly and ran to meet him. "Aurèle, come to play with us. O Aurèle, come and see my daisies!"

"What a pretty chain!" said Aurèle, smiling brightly at the little fellow in spite of his sad thoughts. "But I cannot come and play with you now; I have come to take you home."

"O Aurèle, it can't be bed-time yet. Let us stay out just a little longer."

"Well, you will not go to bed just yet, at any rate. But you must come to Mamma; she wants both you and Guillaume. Come, Guillaume."

"Trouble me not, I am asleep," answered Guillaume, who had not moved. But as he glanced up dreamily, something in Aurèle's face made him give up his idea of plaguing his brother, and he rose to follow him indoors. Here they found Madame de St. Croix wandering restlessly about the chateau. One or two boxes were being carried down, and the children's walking things were laid out in the day nursery, where they expected to find their supper of bread and milk. Henri was with her, but Marie was nowhere to be seen.

"Everything is ready," said Monsieur de St. Croix, advancing from the salon, as they came downstairs again. "Come, little wife, bring the children, and let us eat something before we go."

"Marie! Where is Marie?" asked Madame, as they entered the room. "The poor child has hidden herself. I must look for her."

"I will go, Mamma" said Aurèle, running off before she could answer. He went up to the deserted nurseries and called her, but in vain. She slept in a room by herself, near her mother's; but she was not there. Going to the window, however, he spied a little figure standing by the balustrade at the end of the terrace, and running downstairs again, let himself out by the side door.

Marie did not hear him approach. She was looking dreamily out over the fast darkening landscape, with her eyes fixed on a line of gold which lay along the horizon behind the distant hills — eyes that, as Aurèle could see even in the dim light, were full of tears.

"Marie!" he said gently, as he put his hand on her shoulder.

Marie turned and clung to him, as all his brothers and sisters turned to Aurèle, whether joy or sorrow moved them. "O Aurèle!" she sobbed, hiding her face on his shoulder, "I will be brave, I won't complain; but just now I felt as if I must have one little cry, so I ran out here. It is so strange, so horrible. To go away tonight, without Father Gabriel or anyone, and leave everybody without saying goodbye, and the dogs and everything — our own home that we have lived in ever since I can remember. Oh, it seems as if it would be easier to bear everything here than to go away!"

"Marie, my sister, listen; you do not know how much worse it would be to stay. Could you bear to see rude, rough men knocking everything about, stealing everything they liked, and perhaps making us all prisoners?"

Marie checked her sobs, and listened with wide open eyes of horror. "But, Aurèle, how could they dare? Is not my father De St. Croix of St. Croix? And this his own chateau and his own land? And what evil has he done? Is he not the best man in the world?"

"You know that it is counted wrong to be a Protestant," he said.

"I know you always say so," returned the bewildered girl. "But we have been Protestants all our lives, and nearly every one in the village is a Protestant, and it never made any difference till that dreadful Sunday evening when the strange men came down and shut us out of the church, and Papa said in the evening, when you were talking, that if the worst came we would die for our religion: and Henri and I have always said we would. But it never made any difference, except that we had no more services, and you and Papa have gone away sometimes when we went to bed, somewhere with Father Gabriel. O Aurèle! What does it all mean? What have you been doing?"

"I will tell you what it means, Marie," said Aurèle, as he sat down on the balustrade and put his arm around Marie. "You know, though people did not like Protestants in this country, they used to let us alone, and so we have lived just like other people as long as you and I can remember. In fact, Father says that the Protestants have been let alone ever since the days of Henry the Fourth, who made a law, called the Edict of Nantes, which said that we should be allowed to worship God as we thought right. But last year King Louis thought he was going to die, and he is a Roman Catholic, and they think they ought to stop people from being Protestants, and so he made up his mind to try and make all us Protestants into Roman Catholics again. So he made another law, which said that all our churches were to be shut up, and everybody was to be punished if they did not turn Romanist, and pray to the saints and all the rest that Father Gabriel told you the Romanists do. So when we did not shut up our church, because, as Father Gabriel says, we must obey God rather than man, they sent those strange men down to drive us out; and then they threatened that if we did not stop meeting for our own worship, and go to the mass like the people at Dillon and old Pierre Santon, and the Blancs, and those people here, they would send soldiers to punish us. But we could not do that, you know, because it would not have been right. So every Sunday night, when it gets dark, Papa and Father Gabriel and I, and nearly all the village, have been down into the woods and had our service, so that they should not know it. But they have found out somehow; and a letter came to our father today from a gentleman who lives farther on the Bordeaux road, to say that the soldiers were coming, and we must get away as fast as we could. So we are going to the house where Mamma was born, in the Cévennes."

"What! And leave the house and the poor people and Father Gabriel to the soldiers? O Aurèle! What will they do?"

"It *is* hard" said the boy, and his brave young voice quivered for the first time. "But it must be right; Papa and Father Gabriel said so, and they know best. Little sister, do you know what Papa said to me this afternoon? 'This is our first real trial, let us see to it that we, who have boasted, shall not be found wanting.' "

"Aurèle," said the girl, standing up by herself, and clasping her hands with almost childish solemnity, "I will be brave. I will not be found wanting. Pray for me, Brother."

Aurèle bent down and kissed her forehead. "Yes, Darling," he whispered; "and do you also pray for me, for all of us. And now," he added more cheerily, jumping down from his perch, "let us make haste in, Marie; Mamma will be wondering what we are doing.

In fact they met Father Gabriel just coming out to look for them. Madame de St. Croix was afraid that they would have no time to eat before starting. Not that either of the two children had much appetite; but Marie, following her brother's example, tried hard to eat, though she felt as if each mouthful would choke her. The strange meal came to an end at last, and Madame de St. Croix, who by this time had lost all composure, and was weeping bitterly, hurried them into their outdoor garment and brought them down to the great door, where the travelling carriage was waiting in the yet moonless night. It held Madame de St. Croix and the four younger children; the maid went on the box; and horses were waiting for Aurèle, his father, and the only other servant who accompanied them, a man some years older than Monsieur de St. Croix, who had lived from his birth, so to speak, in the service of the family.

That was a strange, sad night for the poor children, the first of many such. One after another they all fell asleep; even Marie dozed a little, though she woke very often, and always to the same surroundings — the dark carriage interior, where the now risen moon shed a fitful light on Louis's fair hair and Henri's sleeping profile, the dim mysterious landscape outside, and the measured trot of the five horses on the lonely road — so that she felt as if she must have been travelling just so for years.

At last the moon faded again; a pale gray light stole over the country, and Marie, waking from a longer sleep than usual, saw Aurèle bending from his horse to look for her, and point out the rising sun as he came up from the woody horizon and shone upon the silvery mists. By-and-by they passed two or three cottages scattered by the wayside, and at last through a tiny, straggling village where one or two inhabitants, just starting for their early toil stared curiously after the carriage.

At last they came to a small inn at the farther end of the village, and here they stopped for a little while to give the horses water. Poor things! They needed rest, for it was now nearly seven hours since they had left the chateau. They could not, however, stay more than a few minutes, as Monsieur de St. Croix was anxious to accomplish a long journey before noon. A large village, the inhabitants of which were almost entirely Protestants, lay on their route, distant about thirty miles from St. Croix, the curé of which was well known to Monsieur de St. Croix. Here, having come the last six miles at a slow trot, they arrived about twelve o'clock, and here they intended to remain the rest of the day, to start early the following morning.

Indeed, it seemed to Marie that she had only just closed her eyes, when, at five o'clock the next morning, she was roused by Henri calling out, "Marie, come, get up; Aurèle and I are already dressed, and Mamma has been asking for you."

Marie had shared the same room with her mother and Louis, owing to the curé's not having many spare apartments. She had not heard her mother rise and dress. However, she was not very long, considering that she had never been accustomed to wait upon herself, and that Agathe, the maid, was too busy dressing Louis to attend to her. The horses were already being put in when she came down. Her father had gone out, and the rest were still in the breakfast room.

Two whole days they drove in this way with all possible swiftness. On the fourth day, as they again took their places in the carriage, they were told that they should reach St. Louis-de-Linard in the evening.

The morning was lovely, and the drive began very happily; but the August sun soon grew very hot, and the dust sometimes was stifling. Long before the day was over the children grew very tired, and they were all leaning back silent and sleepy, as the carriage crawled wearily up a hill toward evening, when Aurèle rode up to the window with his cap off and called to them to look out. St. Louis-de-Linard lay in the valley almost at their feet, and half a mile of very steep road would bring them to it.

It was a pretty scene. A noisy, sparkling stream ran through the little village, and flung itself over the great wooden wheel of the mill, which stood lower down. It ran close by the walls of the chateau, which was much older and more like a castle than the one they had left. A pretty wooden bridge led to the courtyard gate, and the setting sun made everything look bright.

"It is surely another home, sweet mother," said Aurèle, as he dismounted from his horse to lead it down the hill. Then perceiving that she was struggling to repress her tears, he called away the children's attention, and left the task of consoling her to his father.

The manservant had been sent on beforehand to give notice of their approach, so that a few hurried preparations had already been made by the middle-aged couple who for years had been the only occupants of the chateau; but it still looked bare and desolate to eyes accustomed to the ease and comfort of St. Croix.

Supper was hastily prepared; the tired horses were littered down in the disused stables, and the family gathered in the salon with more cheerful faces than they had worn for some days. Indeed, the younger children were delighted, and coaxed Aurèle to accompany them on a tour of inspection round the premises. They missed him, however, on returning to the house, and would have run out again in search of him, had not Madame de St. Croix, who was sitting by the window with her husband looking now as if nothing had happened to trouble her, suggested that they ought to go to bed.

"How strange it seems to have only one maid, and go to bed by ourselves!" said Marie, as Agathe went off with Louis, and Henri lingered in her room before going to his own. "And *what* a light!" she continued, looking with great disfavour at the feebly-burning lamp which had been placed in her room. "One cannot even see what the chamber is like."

"There's the bed all right, at any rate," said Henri; "and there's a jolly moon coming up over the hill. Look, Marie, how beautifully it shines upon the water!"

The two children stood looking out upon the lovely scene for a few moments, and then Henri wished his sister goodnight, and betook himself to his room. But he had scarcely been gone ten minutes, and Marie had only completed the leisurely brushing out of her long thick hair, when there was a gentle knock at her door, and running to open it, she found Henri outside, still fully dressed.

"Marie," he said," I *cannot* go quietly to bed just yet! It is all so strange and beautiful. Come out again with me, just for a few minutes, and let us see the valley by moonlight."

"Do you think we might?" began Marie, eager, but hesitating.

"What harm can come to us here? Is not Aurèle out by himself still? Mamma sent us to bed because she thought we were tired; but it is not so."

"No indeed; I do not feel that I could sleep."

"Come, then."

And the two children stole quietly downstairs again, slipped through a side door which had not been fastened, and found themselves on the flat irregular terrace of grass which ran round three sides of the chateau, between the wall and the stream. The full moon shone with a flood of light into the little valley, on the now motionless mill-wheel, and the little stream, whose murmur alone broke the stillness of the night; while the dark outlines of the surrounding hills stood out sharply against a cloudless sky.

"Hush! There is a footstep," whispered Henri suddenly, as he drew Marie back into the shadow caused by the angle of the wall.

"It is only Aurèle," murmured Marie, as the next moment their brother came in sight. "O Henri, how beautiful he looks!"

Aurèle was walking bareheaded, with the moonlight on his fair bright hair and sweet, brave face. He seemed full of thought, and did not notice the children standing in the shadow till he came close to them, when he stopped abruptly and seemed to listen.

"It is only us, Aurèle," said Henri, coming out into the light again.

Aurèle made a gesture of surprise. "You, Henri, and Marie! I thought you went in some time ago."

"So we did, but we came out again," replied Marie. "Is it not lovely here?"

"Yes," said Aurèle absently. "Listen," he added; "do either of you hear anything — any other sound than the rushing of the water?"

The three strained their ears in silence for a moment, and then Henri said, "No, there is nothing else."

"But I am almost sure of it," said Aurèle anxiously, still listening.

"Look!" whispered Marie fearfully, laying a sudden hand on Henri's arm.

In the clear full moonlight a figure was distinctly seen to emerge out of the darkness round the corner of the steep road down which they had so lately come — the figure of a man on horseback, followed by another, and another, and another. About twenty of them appeared altogether, riding two abreast down into the valley. The moonlight glistened upon shining steel here and there, and the tramp of horses' feet was now distinctly audible above the ripple of the water.

Aurèle scarcely waited for the appearance of the whole body before he turned to run, and the three made the best of their way into the castle-yard again. At the inner entrance he paused, and spoke in a quick, breathless tone, "Henri, go round to the servants' hall, and tell Pierre and Michelet to go round at once and secure all the gates. Stay yourself at the kitchen door till I join you — Marie, run to the children; help Agathe to dress them, and bring them down to Henri at the same door to wait for me. I shall not be long."

He ran toward the salon as he finished speaking; while Henri and Marie, with the ready confidence in their elder brother which had so often stood them in good stead, hurried off to the different tasks he had given them.

Aurèle entered the room where his father and mother were still sitting. "Father," he said at once, "have you anything that wants hiding carefully? I do not know that there is any danger, but there are soldiers coming down the hill-road."

Madame de St. Croix gave a faint cry, and rose pale and trembling from her seat. "I must go to the children," she said.

"Mamma, indeed the children will be safely hidden," said Aurèle earnestly, "but not if you are with them, and it is best you should not know where. Please trust me, Mamma."

She would not have heeded him; but her husband, who was already leaving the room, turned back to say: "Wait but a moment here, dear Marie; I will return, or call you to them, whichever seems best. Come, Aurèle."

Father and son left the room together and the poor mother sank down in an agony of prayer by the still open window, where the moonlight came in so brightly, so peacefully.

Monsieur de St. Croix hurried on without speaking, till they reached his bedroom where, unlocking one of the travelling bags, he took out a small iron box and a French New Testament, which he put into his son's hands.

"Put them where you will, Aurèle," he said; "I leave them in your charge. Go to your mother when you can; I must see after the men first."

One grasp of the hand, one earnest kiss and blessing, and the father and son parted.

Aurèle rushed upstairs, where he found the boys almost dressed; Marie pale and silent, Louis crying, and Agathe chattering volubly. As soon as they were ready, he sent Agathe to her mistress; and taking Louis by the hand, he ran down the other staircase, followed by Marie and Guillaume.

Henri, true to his orders, was waiting alone at the kitchen door; though he quivered with impatience as the trampling hoofs echoed on the wooden bridge, and a loud voice cried, "Open, in the King's name!"

"This way! Quick!" cried Aurèle, dragging his brothers and sister down a short passage into a sort of inner court, which looked as if no one had been there for centuries. There were lesser buildings and offices within it; an old oven, among others — large enough to contain human beings, as well as loaves — which had fallen into disuse for many years. It had probably been intended, as a secondary purpose, for a hiding-place; for it was so much like the wall of the outhouse itself that it would have escaped general outside observation, while there was a secure fastening on the inside, and a narrow grating high up to admit a scanty supply of air and light.

Aurèle, who had discovered this hiding-place in the course of his thorough examination of the chateau on their first arrival, opened the door, and handed Louis in before the children knew what he was doing. Louis naturally shrank from the dark hole, as it seemed to him, and cried to be taken out. Aurèle took the child into his arms again, and spoke earnestly, "Louis, my darling, listen! And all of you also. There are soldiers coming, and we must all hide till they are gone. This place will just hold you four, and the only thing you can do for Papa and Mamma is to stay here bravely and quietly till they are gone again. Will you do this, dears?"

Guillaume showed his readiness by climbing, without a word, into the great black oven, and Marie held out her hands to her little brother.

"We will be brave and quiet, Aurèle. Come, Louis! You will stay with sister Marie?"

"Get into the oven, Darling Marie," said Aurèle tenderly, "and then I will give him to you."

Marie climbed up with Henri's help, and Louis suffered himself to be lifted into her lap. One earnest kiss passed between Aurèle and his sister, and then he turned to Henri.

"Henri," he said quickly, putting the box and the Testament into his hands, "keep these safe, and do not part with them while you live. Whatever noise you hear, be still and quiet, and keep the bolt shut; see! it goes this way. But if, when the sunlight comes through the grating on the second morning, we do not come, and everything seems quiet, come out carefully. If you do not find us at once, there is money in the box — do the best you can. And take care of the others till we meet again; I leave them in your charge. Goodbye, Henri."

The heavy iron door closed up the poor children in their narrow dark prison, and scarcely waiting to hear the bolt slid back into its place, Aurèle was gone.

He had heard the great gate of the court fall with a crash beneath the repeated blows of the soldiers; he heard their horses' feet clatter on the stones, and fear for his parents gave wings to his feet as he sped along the back passages to gain the salon.

Madame de St. Croix had risen from her knees, and was standing with clasped hands in an agony of apprehension in the middle of the room. As the door burst open, she sprang forward with a cry, and, perceiving that it was her son, eagerly exclaimed, "Aurèle! Your father — the children — tell me where they are!"

"The children are safely hidden, Mamma," replied the panting boy; "no one can hurt them. And Papa will be here directly; I heard his voice as I came along."

"Listen! They are coming!" whispered his mother, with white face and dilated eyes, as the sound of many feet and voices echoed along the unused passages. "Merciful God, save my husband!"

"Hide, Mamma! for Papa's sake, hide! Don't you remember what he said?" exclaimed Aurèle, pushing his mother back. "That cupboard there! It will do until he comes." And exerting all his strength, this strange boy almost forced his mother into a light closet at the farther end of the room, and turned the button upon her.

He had but just time to run again into the middle of the room when the door opened, and in a moment the still, moonlit room seemed to be filled with armed men. They paused for a moment as the slight, boyish figure, with the moonlight on his fair hair and beautiful face, confronted them alone, and the brave young voice made itself heard in the momentary silence.

"What is it that you desire, messieurs? My father will be here in a moment, to know the reason of so strange a visit."

"Your father!" laughed a coarse, brutal tone, as one who seemed in authority among them advanced before the rest; "he has found out our coming and the reason already, to his cost."

A sudden pang shot through Aurèle's heart. His father, then, was perhaps already a prisoner.

"Where is my father?" he cried.

"Where his son will be in a few minutes, unless he has been brought up to know better than to be a traitor," answered the same mocking tone.

"My father is no traitor!" burst forth Aurèle indignantly. "He lies who calls him so."

A storm of curses and threats followed this exclamation, as the soldiers crowded round the boy. It was some time before Aurèle could distinguish anything that was said to him; but at length the same voice broke out, "Why do we stop here and waste words on this spawn of a heretic? Knock him on the head, and let us to the plunder. He is too true a chip of the old block to go free."

"Give him a chance, Captain," interposed one who did not look quite so ferocious as the rest. "Pity France should lose him; he is a fine little fellow."

"You were ever a weak monster," answered the first voice; "but you have my soft side. Answer me, boy," he added, cocking his pistol full in the face of Aurèle, who stood not two yards from him. "Leave these fooleries, come along and lead a brave life with good Catholics; or take your discharge, and see what the next world will do for you."

"He does not understand," put in the second speaker, before Aurèle could answer. "Come, my boy, leave off these heresies, and swear by the mass that you repent of them."

"Never — so help me God!" replied Aurèle, and his face was as the face of an angel.

As the words left his lips, the report of a pistol rang through the room, and without a cry the brave lad fell.

There was a second's intense hush, and the moonlight shone alike upon the rough yet horror-stricken soldiers and the pale, upturned, beautiful face.

Then another sound rang out into the night, a long loud shriek; a closet door burst open with one violent effort, and the poor mother flung herself upon the body of her child. She saw nothing else. She raised the drooping head, and strove to stanch the quickly-flowing blood. It was in vain, all in vain. But she did not cease till the captain of the band, striving to recover his effrontery, advanced and said, "Come, Madame, it is of no use. Ladies should not hide in closets if they wish their presence to be respected. Leave this gloomy room, and I will see that you are cared for."

He even advanced, and would have raised her. But she started to her feet with a gesture which would have made a bolder man pause for a moment, and stood there confronting them with speechless passion — a desperate mother standing over the dead body of her child.

"What have you done with my husband?" she demanded, or rather hissed through her clenched teeth.

There was no answer.

"I ask you, where is my husband?" she repeated in those strange husky tones.

"Never fret for him, Madame," exclaimed the man at length; "we will find you twenty better.

"Shame, shame!" burst from two or three of the men. But Madame de St. Croix neither moved nor spoke. She looked from one to another in silence, and then, with a sudden spring over Aurèle's body, she clutched the throat of the man who had spoken, and with one vigorous unexpected blow sent him reeling to the floor.

By that frenzied act she sealed her own doom. Before any of the men could interpose, before even he had risen to his feet the ruffian hurled his pistol at her head, and she fell senseless and bleeding by her son's side.

II

TWO NIGHTS IN AN OVEN

Meanwhile the four children crouched, shivering and trembling, in the great oven, where there was but just room for their four selves.

Guillaume lay down along the side in his favourite position, with his arm under his head; Marie sat with Louis in her arms, away from the door, and Henri spent his time in fruitless attempts to see something out of the narrow grating just under the oven roof, till Marie begged him to sit still, as she wanted to listen.

They heard the soldiers ride into the yard, and wait, as it seemed, for a few moments' parley, before the sound of trampling feet passed into the castle. And then, in the pause of silence which followed, Henri distinctly heard a sound full of dread and horror — the sharp report of a pistol. Involuntarily he looked at Marie. At the same moment a ray of moonlight straggling through the grating fell upon her face, and showed it to him, pale as death, with dark eyes full of terror.

Neither of them spoke. Marie only pressed Louis to her breast. Poor child, he was already falling asleep again, and they strained their ears, for further sounds. Henri, with his hot forehead pressed against the cold iron door, was doing fierce battle with himself. God only knows how that boy, with his passionate love of his father, mother, and brother, his earnest longing to do something to prove his faith, and his natural love of danger and daring, longed to rush out and join the others — to have some other share in that night's work than to be hidden away with the children. But Aurèle's last words rang in his ears, "I leave them in your charge;" and also a sentence

27

that his father had once bid him remember: "My son, to obey is better than to sacrifice." So he stayed at his post, and by-and-by turned round again to see if he could still see Marie's face.

The moonlight only touched her hair now; all the rest of the oven was in shadow. But he did not think she was asleep. "Marie," he said in a whisper.

"Yes," answered Marie at once.

"Is Louis asleep?"

"Yes, and I think Guillaume also. O Henri! Do you hear them trampling about? I think they must be searching the castle."

"Yes; they are coming out this way. Keep quiet, Marie; they will search these buildings. Pray God that Louis may not wake."

They held their breath as the stumbling feet came round from the back door, and a party of soldiers passed close to the outhouse in which the oven was built. Henri could even hear what they said.

"Come, Jacques, what use to poke about here like a couple of bats, when there is so much to be got in the house? There is no one else about, and for my part, I do not wish to look too closely. Such work is not to my taste."

"Look here!" interrupted another voice, as the feet paused; "here is something of a hiding-place. Hold the light in, and let us see."

Something that was not moonlight flashed for a moment through the narrow grating, and Henri instinctively shrank away from the door.

"There is a door at the end," said the second speaker, and the feet came nearer.

"Bah!" answered the first," it is but an old oven; "and he gave a wrench at the door, which, secured by the inner fastening, did not open. "There, you see," he added, "it is stuck with age." But at the same moment such a blow was struck upon the door that the two boys woke with a start, and Marie's hand closed over Louis' mouth only just in time.

There was a moment of awful suspense, and then the first voice said, "There, it is just as I said, you too curious fellow. Nothing but dust and cobwebs in there, and good drink to be had for nothing in the house. Let us go back and report the work done. For my part, I never heard but that Monsieur de St. Croix had but one boy; at any rate, there are no younger children here."

What the other man answered they did not hear, as the voices and steps receded, and the court grew silent again. The children remained panic-stricken and speechless for some time; but no one came. At length Guillaume heaved a sigh of relief, and settled himself to sleep again without a word. Louis asked Marie in a whisper if they were to stay there all night.

"I do not know, Darling," said Marie, caressing him; "Papa will send Aurèle to fetch us as soon as he can, and we must wait patiently. Don't you think you had better go to sleep again?"

"Don't I hurt you, Marie?" asked the little fellow.

"No, Darling, not at all," answered the girl bravely. She would not confess even to herself that her arms were beginning to ache a little already with their unusual burden.

"Goodnight then," said Louis, reaching up his little face to kiss his sister, and almost immediately falling asleep in her arms.

There was again a long silence, broken by distant sounds and cries which every now and then made themselves heard, but seemed too far away to come from the castle. Marie thought that the soldiers were going away. She could not see her brothers, but she knew that Guillaume and Louis were asleep, and that Henri was huddled in a sitting posture against the door. At length, feeling as if she could no longer bear the silence and darkness, she called to him gently, "Henri, are you awake?"

No answer. She listened attentively for a few moments, and distinguished his breathing as well as that of the other two. She was alone, then, the only one awake. She felt almost inclined to call and wake her brother; but restraining herself, she leant back against the oven wall, and tried to follow his example, but in vain. The slow hours dragged by, and she sat awake till the slow, regular breathing of her three brothers almost maddened her, and she had to pray for help not to wake them, she so longed to do so.

Toward morning everything became quiet; the most distant cries died away, and at length Marie fell asleep herself. She felt as if hours must have passed when she again awoke, and found everything the same, except that now Henri was awake, and she could see through the grating that it was daylight.

"Have you been awake long, Henri?" she asked in a low voice.

"No, not very long," said her brother, "and I have heard nothing since. Give Louis to me, Marie; you must be tired of holding him so long."

"I can wait till he wakes, thank you," said Marie, with a little resolute sigh. "He is happier asleep, and it would wake Guillaume too."

Guillaume here lifted his head for a moment, and looked at Marie, to signify that he was awake.

"Does your head ache, Guillaume?" asked Marie, perceiving, even in the dim light, that his eyes were heavy.

"A little," answered Guillaume.

There was silence for a few moments, and then Marie asked wistfully, "Do you think it will be long, Henri, before they come to let us out?"

"It has not been light very long, I think," answered Henri. "I was trying to measure by the sun. It must have risen above the courtyard wall to come through this grating; but then we look to the east and the sun is up very early now — before five o'clock I heard Agathe say."

"How should Agathe know?" asked Marie, a little scornfully. "*She* never gets up at five and what has that to do with Aurèle? He would not be waiting for the light, but for the soldiers to go. Perhaps they are asleep now, Henri, and that is why everything is so still."

"I daresay we shall hear them going away soon," answered Henri, trying to speak confidently, but with a sinking heart. He understood better than any of the others what great danger they were all in, and found it very hard to do nothing but sit still and wait, without knowing what was going on. They all listened anxiously for two long silent hours, almost without speaking; but no sound came from without, and the stillness began to impress them with great awe: it was like being in a tomb.

At length Louis awoke, and was so much alarmed at the strange place in which he found himself, that it took time to pacify him. But he was naturally a sweet little fellow, and, after the first alarm, began to enter into Marie's desperate attempts to think the whole adventure great fun. He slid out of Marie's arms, and tried, in the narrow prison, to make a nest between his sister and Guillaume, because Marie was tired. He tried to catch the motes in the narrow sunbeam that came through the grating, and his pretty, childish ways did the two elder ones good.

"Marie," he said, stopping short at last, "when are we going to have breakfast?"

"When Mamma or Aurèle comes to let us out," answered his sister. "You shall have breakfast directly then."

"Can't we have breakfast before Aurèle comes?" suggested Louis, with the air of one who has a bright idea.

"No, dear; because, you see, there is nothing to eat here."

"I've got two biscuits," announced Guillaume suddenly. "I kept them for you, Marie; but Louis can have one if he likes."

"Oh, thank you, Guillaume; but, indeed, I don't want anything to eat yet," replied Marie. "Give one to Louis, and eat the other yourself."

"Here, Louis," said Guillaume, getting at his pocket with some difficulty in the crowded space, and giving a good-sized biscuit; but Henri noticed that only one was brought out.

Louis took the biscuit joyfully, and breaking it in two, held out half to Henri.

"No, no," said Henri, pushing it away. "Eat it up, Louis."

"Don't you want it, Henri?" asked the little fellow.

"No, Darling. Marie and I will wait."

Louis folded his little hands together and said grace aloud, as if he had been in the nursery at home, and then began to munch his biscuit with great satisfaction. Henri felt rebuked by the child's simple act, and when Louis had finished, he said, "There is one thing we could do, if we cannot have breakfast. We could say our prayers."

"I've said mine," came from Guillaume's dark corner.

"I wish I had thought of it, too," answered Henri frankly. "Shall we say them together now?"

Guillaume answered by trying to get up and kneel, a proceeding which Louis easily managed, but none of the others could kneel upright. However, they waited in silence for a minute or two, and then Henri, taking courage, began to repeat his usual prayers aloud. After them, he paused. Like all boys, he was very shy of his own feelings, and did not like to say anything special. It was Marie's voice which at length spoke for him, as it were, in a few simple words, "O Father, Thou seest we are in great trouble, and do not know what to do. Help us, we beseech Thee. Take care of Mamma and Papa and Aurèle and take care of us, too, and help us to be patient and good until they come to let us out. For Jesus Christ's sake. Amen."

Then the long hours dragged wearily by as best they might. No one came, no sound was heard; only the sun beat fiercely down upon the oven roof, and the heat became almost intolerable. Louis was flushed and restless, and though not actually fretful, was very uneasy, poor child. At length, to the great relief of the other three, he fell asleep again, resting against Guillaume.

"Cannot you lean back more, Marie!" said Henri. "You look so tired."

Marie gave a wan, faint smile as she tried to do so; but Henri noticed, with alarm, how white she was, and how different from his bright little sister of two days ago. He saw, with relief, that she closed her eyes; but she did not sleep, and her breathing came in short gasps now and then.

"Don't you feel well, Marie?" Henri asked at last.

"It is only the heat," murmured Marie faintly. "It will not last much longer now."

"No; Aurèle is sure to come soon," repeated Henri, in spite of the fears which grew within him.

"Listen!" said Guillaume, moving his little brother's head gently, so that he could see Henri. "Let us play at the game of stories. I will begin."

And he began at once to tell them one of the strange marvellous tales, full of a boy's odd fancy, which he had never told before to any one but Louis. It interested the older children, in spite of themselves, and Louis, when he woke up shortly after, lay quite still in listening content. They made a strange group in that dim, stifling oven: Henri sitting by the door, with his knees drawn up; Marie leaning back against the other end, and touching him with her feet; Louis lying in the midst, with his golden head leaning against the only one whose look and attitude were just the same as they had always been, and whose dreamy voice made a sort of music which helped them to be still all that summer afternoon.

Toward evening Louis asked rather piteously if they were not going out before tea, and Guillaume quietly took out his other biscuit, and gave it to his little brother.

"Aren't you going to have any tea?" asked the puzzled child.

"Not now," answered Guillaume; "that is for you."

"Marie must have some," said Louis, moving nearer to his sister, who had not moved or spoken for some time.

"No, thank you," whispered Marie; but in so strange a voice that Henri exclaimed, "Marie, you will faint! You must eat something!"

"I cannot," answered Marie, with a more painful gasp. "I cannot breathe."

"I will open the door!" exclaimed Henri in great alarm. "We will not wait any longer; it must be safe!"

"No, no!" cried Marie with sudden energy, striving to grasp her brother's arm. "Guillaume, stop him — till the sunlight comes through on the second morning. Aurèle said it."

"But he did not mean you to die, Marie," answered her brother hoarsely.

Louis gave a low cry of terror.

"I shall not die," said Marie's sweet voice, growing faint again as she spoke. "Christians and De St. Croix — Henri, let us be worthy of our name."

But Henri had buried his face in his hands, and his whole frame writhed with the sobs which he *would* not let come. Dearer to him than father, mother, brother, or life itself, was his twin-sister Marie, and never in all his life did he so keenly feel what trial was till then. He did not hear the unwonted caresses and soothing speech from Guillaume which at last quieted Louis enough to eat his biscuit and fall asleep again, nor the sweet childish prayer which he repeated aloud before doing so. After a while he strained his ears to catch Marie's breathing, and thought she was asleep. But Marie did not sleep; in fact, she scarcely even dozed that long night through. Her breath grew short and quick and more than once she thought, in spite of her brave words to Henri, that she must die before the morning came. But at last the moonlight faded, the darkness changed, and the blessed sunlight struck upon the wall once more.

Henri restrained an eager spring when he saw Marie's closed eyes, and thought she was asleep. In a very few moments she opened her eyes.

"Has the light come back?" she asked feebly. "O Henri! Open the door."

Henri needed no second bidding. The bolt went stiffly back again, and the door was pushed open with such violence that Henri fell out as well, and hastily jumped up from the ground, not hurt, but frightened at his own want of caution.

However, no sound came to break the stillness of the sweet summer morning which had now dawned. The sudden change from the stifling gloom to fresh air and sunshine made him giddy; but he soon recovered himself, and held out his arms for Louis. Guillaume already stood by his side, and they helped Louis to get down; but Marie did not move.

"Marie, Marie!" cried Henri in agony, springing back again to his sister's side, and finding her in a dead faint. "Guillaume, help me; she is dying!"

"Stay here, Louis," said Guillaume, as he turned to Henri's help, and between them they got Marie out of the oven, and laid her on the ground, her long black hair trailing in the dust, and her pale, lovely face so changed that even in that moment Henri noticed how different it was to her fresh girlish beauty of three days back.

"See if you can get some water, Guillaume," said Henri hastily. "Go carefully, in case there should still be danger; there is a well in the first court."

Guillaume came back almost immediately with his handkerchief dripping (he had not stayed to look for anything to carry water), and laid it on her forehead. In a few moments she revived, and the sight of Louis, who lay sobbing with his face to the ground, did more to restore her than anything. She stretched out her arms to him, and he crept thankfully to her side. For a moment the four children, still weak and dizzy from their long confinement, sat silently in the rough tumble-down outhouse, where the sunlight fell upon them. Then Marie, with the new sweet gravity which those terrible nights had taught her, said gently, "Let us thank God for bringing us out safely, and then we will try to find the others."

They knelt once more, this time with less difficulty and Henri said a few words of thanksgiving. After this Marie rose, and said, "Louis, Darling, stay with Guillaume till we come back. Henri and I are going to find Aurèle."

Guillaume was going to object to this arrangement. He was the boy; it was clearly his place to go with Henri to explore the castle, and Marie should stay with Louis. But Guillaume scarcely ever spoke without thinking first. He remembered that Henri and Marie had always been together as a matter of course — that Marie would not like to stay behind; clearly, therefore, he must do so. So he sat down again, and began crooning one of his old stories to Louis as they waited.

Meanwhile Henri and Marie crossed the court with trembling footsteps, and approached the kitchen door.

There was no sound of anything alive, nor did anything here look as if it had been disturbed. They entered the castle, and went first into the kitchen. Evidently some one had been there, for everything was in complete disorder — cupboards flung open, in one case even the door had been wrenched from its hinges, and

35

every shelf was bare. A table was overturned, two chairs were broken, smashed and empty bottles lay in every direction, the floor was covered with dirt and litter. Yet no one appeared. There was not even the cat which had spat and growled at Henri when he first passed through the kitchen on that night which seemed now so long ago.

How dreadful, how unbearable that utter stillness grew! With a vague sense of increasing awe, the two children left the room, and crept noiselessly up the staircase, not speaking to each other. In the bedrooms it was the same again. Everything was gone but the bare furniture, which had been too heavy to carry away, and that was broken and flung about in all directions. And here too were the same silence and desolation. Marie tried to call for Agathe, but the word died on her lips, and she dared not mention any other. Slowly they went down the other staircase to the room where they had left their parents, half unwilling to enter, as doubtful what they might find.

Poor things! poor children! What was it that they did find when at last they opened that door and stood upon the threshold? Two figures, lying prone upon the floor, with white upturned faces, in the morning sunlight. Their own mother, still and wounded, with Aurèle's head upon her breast. Marie rushed forward with a shriek, which might have been the echo of her mother's own, and flung herself upon the floor beside them.

"Henri, Henri, help me!" she cried. "See, she smiles! She is not dead!"

It was the smile of death; but Marie had never looked upon the dead before. Henri came, but only to stand helpless, horror-struck, speechless, knowing too well what this must mean.

"Mother! Mother! Mother!" wailed the frantic child — "Henri, lift Aurèle's head — bring water — run!"

Henri knelt down on the floor beside her. "It is of no use," he said in a choked voice. "O Marie, she is dead! — they are both dead!"

She stared at him with wild, unbelieving eyes, and then throwing herself upon the floor, the saving tears came to her relief, and she wept passionately. Henri sat still, like one stunned. He did not even try to comfort her; he did not speak until she raised herself, after some minutes, and cried out passionately, "O Henri! — Father! Let us find him."

"Do you think he is alive, if these two are lying here?" asked Henri hoarsely, almost savagely.

"No, no," sobbed Marie; "but I must see him. Come with me, Henri."

They went by one consent to the great door which led into the outer courtyard. There, on the steps, as he had fallen, and half covered by the corpse of his old servant, lay Monsieur de St. Croix, pale — cold — dead.

It was only what they had expected; but Marie's weeping became almost hysterical, and Henri ground his teeth as he knelt down on the blood-stained stone, and with difficulty moved the body of the servant to one side. Then they knelt, motionless and silent, except for Marie's sobbing, for more than one long horrible moment.

"Henri," said Marie at last, trying to speak calmly, "I must go and tell Guillaume what we have found, and then you and I must do what we can. We must bring water — and she broke down again, but went on, sobbing — "and after that we must let Guillaume come to see them, but not Louis — he need never know all about it. She did not wait for an answer, but went away through the courtyard, crying bitterly, leaving Henri kneeling silently by his father's body.

All this time Guillaume, who, in spite of his cool resolution, was old enough to be terribly anxious, waited in the sunny out-building, trying to amuse Louis, but giving up the attempt at last, and listening only for sounds from the castle. At last, when he had begun to feel almost desperate, he heard Marie's voice calling him from round the corner of the wall, and bidding Louis wait where he was, he rushed out.

Alas! Marie's tears and her blood-stained dress spoke too plainly. Guillaume's eager question died upon his lips; he turned deadly pale, and staggered back against the wall. At last he managed to gasp out, "Who, Marie — who? Not all!" he cried, as she did not answer. "Mamma, Father, Aurèle — O Marie, all?" and Marie only answered by her tears.

At last she spoke, however, and said, "Will you stay with Louis yet a little, please, Guillaume? I cannot come to him like this. Do not tell him, and as soon as I can I will come back, and you shall go to see them."

Then she turned and went away again, and Guillaume did not move till Louis' voice, impatiently calling for Marie, roused him to go to his little brother and try to quiet him.

That day went by like a confused, hideous dream. Together the twins washed away the terrible stains from those dear forms, and composed them as well as they could. Then Marie came back, sad and tearless, to the out-house, and took Louis into the least disturbed of the bedrooms, where she had agreed to wait till Guillaume and Henri came back to her. Louis, not too miserable to think of hunger, asked piteously for food, but she could find none.

Guillaume and Henri were so long away that Marie grew very anxious, and listened at the head of the stairs for any sound in the still, deserted house. They had found nothing but those four dead bodies. There was no sign of Agathe, or of the other two.

At last a door opened, and Henri came quickly up the stairs.

"Marie," he said in a low earnest tone, "go down to Guillaume, in there. I can't get him away."

Marie went downstairs without a word, and Henri hurried in to Louis, who, in spite of his naturally sweet temper, had now, through hunger and alarm, become extremely fretful. He took the poor child on his knee, and sat down by the window.

"I want Mamma — I want Agathe — I want some breakfast!" wailed Louis. The piteous cry was too much for his brother, and did what all the preceding horrors had failed to do. Henri burst into tears, and Louis roused himself with wide-open eyes and suspended sobs. "Henri, Henri!" he cried, "O Henri, I will be good! Don't cry. Are you hungry too?"

"Listen, Louis," said Henri, striving to check his sobs. "The wicked soldiers have taken everything away, and Papa and Mamma and Aurèle are gone too."

"But they will come back again," answered Louis, with a puzzled air. "Mamma won't leave us here all by ourselves; she will soon come back."

"Ah, no! They will never come back," sobbed Henri. "O Mamma, Mamma!"

III

SELF-HELP

It was late in the afternoon before the four children were able to talk calmly over their position. Henri had not forgotten the packet, or book, committed to his care; but for the rest, they had thought of nothing. Clearly the first thing was to get something to eat, but how?

"We must go to the village," said Henri, after a pause. "They may have food there to give us, and shelter, for it is too late now to do anything till tomorrow."

"Oh yes; let us go to the village," said Marie, almost eagerly. "I had forgotten the people there; this place is all so strange."

So they went downstairs into the kitchen, and out by the side door, fearful of again passing by that other way. This brought them out on the other side of the castle, and, in order to reach the bridge, they had to pass round the wall. As they turned the corner, a fresh cry of grief and surprise broke from them on seeing the ruined state of the little valley.

The mill-wheel had stopped. There was still no sound, except the running of the water. Four out of the five cottages lay in one heap of smoking ruins; the fifth, which stood a little apart, showed no sign of life. After that first cry, they proceeded silently. They had gone through sights already which made them feel just then as if nothing else could matter. It was only what they expected, to find the same desolation and disorder in the one remaining cottage as in the castle. Not quite so great indeed, for the scanty furniture remained, though it was thrown about in every direction, and in the cupboard Marie found a jug of milk and half a loaf of bread. Evidently the soldiers had not thought it worth while to look there. All the inhabitants were gone. Probably they had taken refuge in the mountains until the soldiers were gone.

"Don't you think we might have this?" asked Marie, as she took out the bread and milk, and put it on the bare wooden table.

"Yes," said Henri decidedly. "If they come back, we will pay them for it, and tonight we will sleep here."

"There is only one bed," said Marie, doubtfully.

"Guillaume and I will stay in this room. It is quite warm enough to sleep on the ground."

Marie was busy cutting slices from the loaf, and pouring some of the milk into a mug. The children tasted it languidly at first; but their hunger at last made itself felt, and the two boys, at any rate, ate almost ravenously.

"We had better save a little for the morning," said Marie at length, "in case we should not be able to get anything more."

Henri stopped in the act of pouring out fresh milk from the jug, and rose to put it back again. It was now about six o'clock, but they felt as if weeks had passed since they watched for the sunlight in the morning. They sat about in silence for a little while, feeling too sad and listless to do anything.

At last Marie roused herself. "We had better go to bed early tonight," she said. "Come, Louis, you are nearly asleep now. Don't you want to get your things off, and feel nice and comfortable again?"

"You can't undress me," said Louis, opening his eyes wide.

"Oh yes, I think I can," said Marie, too sad to smile at this speech. "And you ought to be washed too. There's no hot water; but such a lovely hot day you'll like cold, shan't you? That wooden tub — Henri, could you and Guillaume get me some water in it? There is an old bucket lying outside.

The two boys rose at once, glad to have something found for them to do. Louis did not at first like the idea of being washed in a wooden tub, but he at last agreed, and then became quite amused at all the new things that he and Marie were trying to do.

Marie found a clean though coarse child's nightdress in a box belonging to the bedroom, and persuaded Louis to wear it. He had just risen from saying his prayers at her knee, when the two boys, whom Marie had asked to look for wood to light a fire with in the morning, returned.

"Why, Louis, how nice and clean you look!" said Henri, laying down a bundle of sticks on the hearth.

"Doesn't he," said Marie eagerly. "I have done everything except brush his hair out; but I can't find anything to do that with."

"They did not take our brushes and combs up there, anyway," said Guillaume, pulling one out of his pocket; "and I brought mine, as you said we might stay here tonight."

Louis was soon in bed, and fell asleep almost directly. Meanwhile Henri and Guillaume went down to wash at the stream, and then filled the tub with fresh water for Marie in the morning.

Marie went out into the yard behind. There was a little heap of straw there, and she meant to bring some into the outer room for the boys to lie on. Her foot struck against something in the straw, and stooping down she found a hen with its head cut off, and two eggs lying close by. She called Henri to look at it.

"Do you think it would be good to eat?" she asked, shrinking a little as Henri took it up.

"Yes; I do not think it has been dead long," said Henri. "Perhaps the soldiers killed it yesterday. Only, how shall we cook it?"

"I don't know how, but I will try tomorrow," said Marie bravely. "I am sure all the feathers ought to come off. We will pull them off, you and I, when Guillaume's bed is made."

Accordingly, when Guillaume had fallen asleep on his straw couch in the kitchen, and the sun was getting low, Henri and Marie sat down on a log of wood by the door to pluck the hen. For the first time, too, they began to talk of what they must do on the morrow.

"You have the packet safe, have you not?" said Marie. "Perhaps there is something in that to tell us."

Henri took the packet out of its hiding-place in his breast, and opened it with reverent fingers. "All different papers," he said, when the outer covering was taken off, "except this one packet, which feels like money. Let us see what we can make out of them."

Some of the papers the children were too young to understand the value of. There were certificates of marriage, and of the birth of each child. There was a paper containing a list of title-deeds, and a note added, in their father's hand, to say where they had been concealed. There was a letter to an English name in Hampshire, which puzzled them as much as all the rest; one to a French name in Amsterdam, and lastly, there was a hurried note, in their father's hand, written on the back, "For my eldest son after I am dead."

Henri broke down as he finished reading this, and Marie also was quietly weeping.

"What shall I do with it?" he said in a faltering tone. "It was meant for Aurèle."

"You — you are the eldest son now," answered Marie, between her sobs. "Read, Henri; it will tell us what Papa meant us to do."

It was very short, and had been written in such haste that they could hardly read it.

> If we should be taken from you on our way, make your way to the coast, and go as secretly as you can to Amsterdam — not to England, as I had meant. You will find money enclosed, and a letter to a lady there, who will receive you for our sake. Love each other, and whatever happens, be in the true faith which we have taught you. And may the good God bless and keep you, my children, until we meet again!
>
> — Your loving father and mother,
> Louis and Marie De St. Croix.

Marie's busy fingers did not cease from her work, but her tears were falling fast upon the dead bird. Henri refolded the paper in silence.

They counted the money in the paper, and found that there were seventeen gold pieces, each worth twenty-five francs, and five francs in silver. "Four hundred and thirty francs," said Marie. "O Henri, how much money!"

"I dare say we shall not find it more than enough," said Henri. And indeed he spoke truth; for on the very day on which they reached St. Louis de Linard, Monsieur de St. Croix had intended to enclose notes to the value of some thousand pounds. "It will take us a long time to get to the sea, and we must keep enough to pay for being taken over."

"I hope we shall not be robbed," said Marie in an awestruck voice.

"We will not let any one know how much we have," said Henri. "See, Marie, you shall take these five francs to spend, and when they are gone I will give you more, and then you can always say you have not got any more."

Marie drew out her silk purse, which contained about three francs still of her last monthly allowance, and put the money into it.

"Ah!" said Henri, when he saw the purse, "I have nearly five francs left in my purse, and I think Guillaume has some, Marie, if you consider. I am afraid this money must be very little. You and I have had ten francs a month, and Guillaume five — that makes twenty-five, just as much as there is in one of these gold pieces, so that we have seventeen months' pocket-money, as one may say; but then, you know, we never bought anything to eat or to wear."

"Ah, well, one can but do one's best," returned his sister, taking up her work again. "O Henri! I don't believe this chicken will ever be done."

"O dear, how thoughtless of me! I have not been helping you," said her brother, beginning to pluck the feathers at such a rate that between them the bird was soon left bare.

"There," said Marie, rising with a sigh of relief. "Now it is all ready to cook tomorrow."

"Are you sure?" asked Henri, doubtfully. "Isn't there some part of the bird's inside that ought to be pulled out?"

"How should I know?" asked Marie, a little proudly. "I am no serving-maid."

"Yes; but I think there is," persisted Henri. "I saw Louison doing it once, and I think I can manage it, give it to me, Marie; you cannot do it."

"No, no, Henri," exclaimed Marie, with a sudden recollection of her pride of birth. "You, De St. Croix of St. Croix, soil your hands with our dinner! It will do just as well without."

"No, it won't; it will spoil it. We may have worse things to do than this," said Henri gloomily. "But," and his bright smile came back again, "one is not the less noble, and rather more De St. Croix."

Marie gave up the bird in silence, and he manfully accomplished his disagreeable task. Then the two brave children, upon whom the care of all was now to rest, said their prayers together, and laying themselves upon their rude couches, which were now a luxury, slept the sleep of God's beloved.

IV

THE PILGRIMAGE BEGUN

Marie was the first to awake next morning, and with some difficulty recalling where she was, raised herself in bed to take a survey of things in general. The sun was shining brightly through the uncurtained window, and as it had not yet risen very high, she supposed it must be early. Louis was still sleeping soundly beside her, and through the door, which she had not been able to fasten the night before, she could see that Henri and Guillaume were sleeping also.

Marie crept quietly out of bed, and managed to wash and dress without awaking the others. Then she went into the outer room, and began to try and light the fire with the sticks and straw which Henri had put ready over-night. She had never done such a thing before. But, in spite of her French nobility, she was beginning to think it was very interesting to have to do everything for themselves, though much more difficult than, if she had ever troubled her head about the subject, she would have thought possible. She managed to get the wood laid on the hearth in some sort of order, and then, after a long hunt for the tinder-box, she began to try and strike a light. This she could not manage at all, and after twice hitting her fingers, she made so much noise that Henri started up from his straw, and was on his feet before he had quite made out what had disturbed him.

"Marie, what are you doing?" he exclaimed, almost indignantly, "letting me lie asleep here, and trying to light the fire yourself!"

"I must begin to be useful now," said Marie, gladly giving up the box into his hands. "I thought it would be such fun to have the fire

46

lighted and everything ready before you woke. I must see how you do it first."

The fire was soon burning away merrily, though it smoked more than the children had been used to. Henri carried Guillaume off to the river again; while Marie hung the fowl in front of the fire by a string from a great nail which was evidently there for the purpose, and then woke Louis, and made him ready for breakfast.

Every one was ready for breakfast before the breakfast was ready for them. The children had had no idea how long it took to roast a chicken. They soon found out that the string must be kept turning, to prevent the chicken from getting burned, and they put an earthenware dish under it to catch the gravy. But the chicken did not seem at all inclined to turn brown.

"What shall we do, Henri?" said Marie, rather dolefully. "I don't believe it will be done for another hour yet."

Henri looked up from the window, where he had been leaning in silent thought for some minutes. "We must wait — that is all," he said, hopefully, "and do now what we should have done afterwards. I have been thinking," and his tone quivered in spite of himself, "that we must go up to the castle again before we leave the valley. We must look over what is left, and see what can be taken with us. Also, I remember a map which my father used to study, and on which he marked the way to the coast, and told me how to understand it. I do not think the soldiers would be likely to take that away, and it might help us, as I do not know which way we ought to go from here to reach the coast. So I will go at once, and I dare say the chicken will be ready by the time I come back."

"I will come with you," said Guillaume, getting up.

"Do you like to do so?" asked his brother, looking at him tenderly.

"Yes." And the two brothers went away together.

It was nearly an hour before they came back, and Marie, who had watched the chicken anxiously, was beginning to think it would be burned, when she saw them returning. Guillaume looked very white; but they were both talking calmly, and each carried a small bundle. At first they did not seem hungry, though they had had nothing for two days except that scanty meal the night before; but Marie pressed them to eat, and when they had once begun, their appetites soon returned. After breakfast they got out the map, which Henri had found thrown aside in his father's room, and tried to make out their journey. The others, who had never seen it before, could not understand it; but Henri was soon able to show them the Chateau de St. Croix and the one which they had just left. Then he found a line, traced evidently by his father, which led from this valley to the sea-coast.

"And now," he said, "we can be in no difficulty for we have only to ask the way from one place to another that lie along the line. The next place from here, you see, is St. Etienne, so we will ask the way to that, and when we get there, we will ask our way to St. Germin, and so on till we come to Bordeaux, where the line ends."

"But," objected Marie, who had tried hard to follow her brother, "how do you know which end of the valley to go out of? There is only one road, and we came by that, and we do not want to go back again."

Henri looked puzzled. "I dare say we shall have to go back a little way, and then turn off," he said; "but I do not know which way we should turn certainly, and there is no one to ask here."

"Couldn't you tell by the sun?" put in Guillaume; who had not spoken before.

"By the sun? Yes. What a good idea!" said Henri, jumping up and running out of the cottage, where the four children had been sitting deep in discussion. "That must be the east where the sun is now, and we must go to the west; then turn with the sun on our right hand, and there is our way. It is that very road."

This point happily settled, they prepared to set out as soon as possible. Two small bundles were made up, which Henri and Guillaume meant to carry. Guillaume had a clean shirt for each, and pocket handkerchiefs — too great a luxury for the peasant children they meant to represent — and a brush and comb which articles they had all agreed were indispensable. Henri had a blanket, in the midst of which was rolled up another brush and comb, and the Testament, out of which he had read to them that morning, and between the leaves of which he had placed, unknown to any one but Marie, three locks of hair — golden, black, and brown. Marie carried the precious map and the remains of the chicken, which she had packed up as tidily as she could, with a knife and fork which Henri had brought from the castle.

It was not much past ten o'clock by the time all was ready, though they thought it was much later as they had been up nearly four hours. At Henri's suggestion, he and Guillaume had taken two clean though coarse blouses which they had found in the cottage, and put them on above their own garments, which were handsome enough to have attracted attention. Marie could only pin a large cotton handkerchief across her shoulders, and take a straw hat made in the fashion of the province, which must have belonged to the woman of the house. They had not the least idea what might be the value of the things, but they left five francs in a little packet on the table, in case the poor people should return.

In this fashion they went up the steep road which led out of the valley. On reaching the corner they turned with one consent to take a last look.

How still and peaceful everything looked! The sun shone between the mountains on the fresh green turf and the water that ran across it, and the castle lay beneath them as tranquilly as if it had never known a scene of violence. But the ruined heap where the four cottages had been told its own tale, and the open window in the castle showed that dreadful room in which Aurèle and their mother were even now lying dead. Tears streamed down their cheeks, and for some minutes no one spoke.

Then Henri took off his cap, and lifting up his face to heaven, said aloud, "Lord, Thou knowest it all; have pity upon us, and watch over us! Go Thou forth with us, our Father, and keep us for ever true Soldiers of the Cross, for Jesus' sake!"

"Amen!" breathed his brother and sister, and turning away, they passed out of sight of the valley in which they had lost all.

In this manner these four children set forth together, trusting in God.

V

A RACE WITH THE DRAGOONS

On a fair August evening, some three days after the events related in the last chapter, the sun was shining brightly down a lovely by-lane — one of those with broad grass borders which here and there in flowery corners spread out into inviting resting-places.

In one of these green nooks, where broad, flat stones were tumbled on the sward, and a little rivulet ran round it on its hurrying way to join a river nearby, the four children were seated round a small fire of sticks — lighted, not for heat, but for the purpose of cooking. Five fish, the result of half an hour's patient angling, with such rude hook and line as Henri could contrive, in the river lower down, were broiling on a small flat stone round which the fire was heaped. Henri might well look with pride at those fish; for not only had he caught three of them with his own hand, but he had also cleaned them ready for cooking, having discovered that it was necessary the day before, when two fish which they had managed to catch turned out unfit to eat. Certainly these young people were learning many things which their nobility would at one time have despised. And they did not look the worse for it either. Marie was the most changed since those happy, careless days, scarcely more than a week ago; but it was a change that suited her, and made her, if anything, prettier than before. Guillaume was lying on the grass in his favourite position half asleep, and Louis was making a daisy chain, as he had last done in the garden at home. They had walked some ten miles that day, and had earned their rest. The way had been lovely, but very tiring, as it lay chiefly along unfrequented mountain-paths. Only once had they passed through the outskirts of a village, and had scarcely dared to do more than ask the way to St. Etienne of a young peasant girl, who was going higher up the mountain with a flock of goats. That was early on the first day after leaving St. Louis-de-Linard, and she had said St. Etienne must be — well it might be twenty, it might be twenty-five miles away. Henri, while the fish were cooking, studied his map deeply; he felt sure they must be near.

"Come, Henri," said the others at last; "the fish are ready: let us have our supper." Henri put up the map carefully, and took out the fish, which were soon eaten. They had had but slender food these three days, and, for the first time in their lives, the boys had known what it was never to have as much as they could have eaten. Yet not even little Louis had been heard to complain.

It did not take long to arrange themselves for the night. They felt it quite a natural thing to sleep out of doors by this time, and in the warm, dry weather had found it rather pleasant than otherwise. Henri, who was making up the fire for the night, turned round in surprise at hearing an exclamation of annoyance from his sister. "What is it, Marie?" he asked.

"Oh, it is so silly, Henri! But my hair gets worse and worse. I never knew how difficult it was to brush ones own hair before! Don't you think I could cut it off with the knife?"

She made such a pretty picture as she said this, sitting on a large gray stone by the flickering wood fire, her cheeks hushed in the summer twilight with the efforts she had made, and the rebellious hair falling in a wavy black mass almost to the ground. But Henri did not stop to notice this, in his horror at her suggestion. "Cut off your hair, Marie!" he exclaimed. "Why, what a fright you would look! There is no one else with hair like yours."

"But it tries me so, Henri, after we have walked nearly all day, and I cannot arrange it at all; it just hangs down and curls anywhere."

"I like it best so," said her brother; "and you shall not have the trouble of brushing it. I am not tired, and it will amuse me to be your lady's-maid." So saying, he took the brush out of her hand, and set to work, in spite of Marie's remonstrances.

It took him more time than he thought, and Guillaume and Louis fell asleep while he was brushing; but at last it was all smoothed out, and Henri began to plait it. "I can plait most things, so I think I can plait hair," he said. "I will make it in two tails for the night, but it must be undone in the morning, and if it gets into a tangle, I will brush it out every night."

"O Henri, you ought not to have to do that," said Marie, the tears springing to her eyes. Somehow that Henri should have to brush her hair impressed their fallen fortunes upon her more than ever. Even when Henri laughed at her, and spoke cheerfully about their journey, she could scarcely smile in answer, and lay awake longer than usual that night with a sore longing for her mother.

It was a warm, still night, and by-and-by the moon rose over the neighbouring wood, and shone full upon Marie's face, so that she edged nearer to one of the fallen stones. As she lifted her head to see if Henri and Guillaume were in shadow, a sound far away upon the road caught her attention, and she listened intently. She was not long in doubt, for it was a sound she was never likely to forget — the distant tramp of approaching horsemen.

With a sudden terror she sprang up, and roused Henri. He listened for a moment, and then said: "They are certainly horsemen, Marie, and I think they are coming this way. I don't know that we are in any danger, but it will be safer to hide till they have passed."

He roused Guillaume as he spoke, and took Louis up in his arms, directing the others to follow him into the field, which was screened from the road by a thick hedge. They had not left the nook many moments, when loud talking and jesting became audible, and directly afterwards a troop of horsemen came round the corner of the lane. They did not seem in any particular hurry; indeed, it would have been difficult to ride fast down this rough, winding lane. One of the horses stumbled as they drew near, which called forth an oath from its rider, a dark, swarthy man, who seemed to be leader among them.

"Look here, sergeant," said one of the men, drawing rein as he pointed to the smouldering fire, "someone has passed down this way lately."

"Some pack of vagabonds or gypsies, most like," said the first carelessly. "They are thick on all the roads, and this is not a likely way for fugitives."

"Tramps would not have fled for us, and when they light a fire, they generally stay the night in a place," muttered the other, dismounting. "I'll have a light to my pipe, at any rate."

Several of the others dismounted for the same purpose, and sat down on the stones to fill at their leisure, while the sergeant and about a dozen of the men waited for them on horseback. Evidently the discipline among the troop was of the loosest.

"How much longer do you fellows mean to loiter?" he asked at last. "One would think we had nothing to do but to go to sleep tonight."

"No; that is what the people of La Verraye are thinking," answered one, with a grim laugh. "They don't think what a capital bonfire we shall treat them to; not they. But never fear, sergeant, we have plenty of time before us. It is not nine yet, and we have scarce two miles to go."

"But you forget that these two miles are along this beast of a road," answered the sergeant, with another oath. "We shall not get beyond fool's pace all the way, unless you wish to ruin another horse tonight."

At this moment Guillaume felt a touch on his arm, and turning, saw Henri with his finger on his lip, and his face full of intelligence. He just breathed the words, "Wait for me here," and slipped noiselessly away along the hedge.

Marie did not see him go, but the next moment she found out that he was not there, and looked at Guillaume with a face full of alarm. Guillaume nodded cheerfully, and signed to her to keep silence. In his heart he knew that Henri had gone on the chance of being able to find and warn the villagers of La Verraye before the troop could reach it, and he was divided between fear for his brother and a longing to run after him. But he knew he must not leave Marie and his little brother, so he only watched more anxiously the movements of the horsemen.

Henri had not been gone two minutes, when the sergeant insisted more peremptorily that they should go on, and accordingly the horsemen climbed again into their saddles, and slowly disappeared — slowly, not only because of the badness of the road, but because it was not wide enough, except just at this corner, for them to ride more than two abreast.

The two children — for Louis had fallen asleep again during their hiding — did not venture to move till the last footfall had died away. Then Marie exclaimed, in a frightened gasp, "O Guillaume, where is Henri?"

"All right, Marie; he will be back directly," answered Guillaume cheerfully. "Can we carry Louis back without waking him, do you think?"

Marie rose with Louis in her arms, and between them they managed to carry the sleepy little fellow back again to his nest in the shadow of the stones without actually awaking him, though he roused himself for a moment to say, "Goodnight, Marie."

Marie cowered beside him in silence, with her face hidden, and Guillaume stood irresolute beside her for some moments. Then Marie lifted up her white, anxious face, and said, "He is gone to find La Verraye, and tell them. Did he tell you so?"

"No; I only guessed it," answered Guillaume, and there was silence again, — a long silence, which seemed as if it would never come to an end. The sweet summer night seemed absolutely without sound, and the utter stillness made the suspense worse. Guillaume asked Marie once if she would not at least lie down while they waited; but she only shook her head, and he sat down on the stone beside her.

Some hours — Marie would have said some weeks — must have passed in this way, when Guillaume fancied that, quite in the distance, he heard sounds, and mounted on the highest stone to look over the hedge in the direction where the village must lie. Marie looked up, and asked if he saw anything.

"Yes," answered Guillaume in a low tone; "there is a red flush in the sky over there, and a little dark cloud against it, that looks like smoke. But it is not much, Marie; it is very little."

Marie, however, was already standing beside him, and together they watched the dull, ominous red which told of distant fire, and strained their ears to catch any sound. But there was none, though on such a night, as Marie said, it should have been easily heard.

"See, the red light is growing fainter," said Guillaume at length. "You see it is not a very big fire, Marie."

"Look there! There is another!" exclaimed Marie in a startled tone, as she pointed to the horizon in quite a different direction.

Guillaume looked, and his instant relief enabled him to laugh, as he replied, "Why, Marie, that is the sunrise. Don't you see what a different red it is, and there is a sort of gray light beginning to come over everything?"

A kind of awe fell upon the two children as they watched that slow increase of light which seems like the gradual lifting of a veil from the earth's face, till the smile of the sun breaks suddenly upon it, and we see again the countenance of an old friend. Louis stirred in his sleep, and called for Marie, who sprung down instantly to soothe him. As she turned to Guillaume some minutes afterwards, she was struck by his listening attitude, and the next instant she herself heard the sound of rapid footsteps in the lane. Before she could say anything, Henri sprung, panting and breathless, into the corner, and threw himself down upon the grass, too much spent at first to do anything but nod in answer to their repeated questions.

"Yes, yes, every one is safe!" he exclaimed at last, in answer to a fresh inquiry from Marie. "I was only just in time, though. I never had such a run in my life."

He sat up as he spoke, and tossed back his hair with the glad boyish excitement which the late terrible events had apparently almost crushed out of him.

"Oh, Marie," he went on, with quick, eager speech, "you can't think how splendid it was! I had a good start, you know, and I knew I should do it; though the road got so smooth toward the end that I expected every moment to hear them close behind. As it was, I heard their voices once, and didn't I run! I came to the village at last, and the road ran straight into it, so I thought it must be La Verraye. It is only one street, as far as I could see; but that was still as death. Only in one house I saw a light. I dashed up to it, and threw a handful of stones at the window. I could even hear a sort of rustle inside, and then the light was moved away, and a man opened the window and asked who was there. 'Quick, for God's sake!' I called out. 'The dragoons are close at hand, and mean to surprise the people of La Verraye tonight.' He shut the window, and in a second it seemed the door was opened, and the same man came out. He was one of our ministers, and there were three other men and a boy. The boy ran off at once up the street, rousing every one up, and before I had got my breath almost, there was a crowd round us. Such a crying and calling! And I all the while fearing that the dragoons would come in the middle. But the minister stopped all that in a minute. Such a splendid fellow, Marie! You must see him. I scarcely heard what he said, he spoke so gently; but we all seemed to understand what was to be done directly he had spoken. The men took the children, and we got them and the women away into the wood at the back of the village. We just saw the last lot safe into the wood, and then the minister said he should see if he had time to take something out of the church. I don't know what it was; but some of those dragoon fellows are the most awful thieves! There were three of us with him — I and two of the men who had been with him first. We got close to the church; but the dragoons came galloping up the street, and they would have been upon us in another minute. There was a sort of moat round the church, deep and almost dry, with thick overhanging bushes. We ran down there and hid; so that, though they could not see us, we could see them pretty well — yes, and hear them too. They battered at the doors, and shouted, and broke into half the houses in the street, before they guessed the truth. Oh, what a rage they were in! It was awful to hear them swear. Then they clustered together in the street, and quarrelled about what they should do next. And some of them wanted to go into the wood after the people; but they knew it was no use — the horses could not do it. At last they settled to go on somewhere; but they still lingered a few minutes. We could not see what they were doing; but all at once, as they turned their horses, one of them threw a great blazing bundle right on to the thatch of the nearest house. 'They shall find the place too hot to hold them when they come back, at least!' he said, with a horrible laugh. O Marie! One of the two men started up, and I saw his black eyes flash with such a look! He would have sprung out; but the minister laid his hand on his arm, and just said a word, and he let himself be drawn down again. But, oh! His head went down between his knees, and his shoulders shook as if he would have sobbed. They said afterwards it was his mother's house. And then another of the fiends laughed out, and flung another firebrand on the house on the other side. 'We shall teach them a lesson, at any rate,' he said, and then we saw the houses burning, as they rode laughing down the street. They had scarcely turned the corner before we were out and at work. They did not guess we were so near; they meant the whole village should burn before we came back. But we worked as I never worked in my life, and a great many of the men came back to help us; so that we got the fire under before it had gone further. The next houses were smoked, and some of the thatch burned off one, but not much harm was done. But only the four walls of the second cottage were left, and the first is as bare as the homes we saw in the valley of St. Louis-de-Linard!"

There was a keen ring of pain, almost a wail, in his voice as he ended; but the next instant the boyish tones came back once more, as he burst out again: "Oh, such a splendid fellow, Marie! He worked like ten men. You must come and see him. I could not come away till the fire was out; but by that time half the people were back in their houses again, and I told the minister that I must go. 'Will you not stay a little while with us?' he said, so kindly. 'I am going to call the people for a thanksgiving service almost directly; after that, I shall so much like to see you at my house, and know more of you.' So I told him something of our story — not our names — and said I must go back to you, because you would be frightened for me. And he told me to bring you all to his house, and he and his sister would do all they could for us, and would be proud to have us, for he said I had saved all their lives. O Marie! To think of having saved his life! Come on! Let us get there as soon as we can."

"But, Henri, you must be quite tired out," said Marie. "Won't you rest before you walk all that way again?"

"I don't feel as if I could," said the boy, kissing her affectionately. "Have you been very anxious about me?"

"I am thankful to have you safely back," said Marie fervently. "Shall we go, then, Henri. See, Louis is just waking again! Can you walk now, Darling?" she asked of the little boy, who was sitting up, and looking about him with wondering blue eyes.

"I should like some breakfast," he said, rather plaintively.

"But we haven't got any here, dearest Louis," said Marie. "See, then, if you can walk a little way down the lane. Henri has found a kind man, who will give us some breakfast — real breakfast in the house. Shouldn't you like that?"

"Yes; Louis will go," answered the small boy, getting up with a resigned air.

"Shall Guillaume carry you some of the way on his back?" asked that person, as he knelt down in front of the child.

This proposal was eagerly accepted, and in spite of the fears expressed by Marie and Henri that Louis would be too heavy for him, Guillaume managed to carry him quite half-way down the uneven lane. When they came near the village they halted; Guillaume set down his burden, and they made themselves look as tidy as they could. Marie brushed out Louis' fair curls, and bathed his face, and Henri opened out the roughened plaits which had kept Marie's hair from tangling all night, and dusted his own jacket and Guillaume's as well as he could. After all, they felt very shy of appearing before anyone as guests in their present trim. But, as Henri said, it was no use stopping to think about it; so they went on into the village.

The street was wide awake and astir now, at any rate. The whole population seemed to have just poured out from the doors of the church, and now stood in little groups about the scene of the principal mischiefs, gesticulating, and deploring, in shrill French voices, the misfortune which had happened to them.

A little apart from one of these groups, and talking to a little old woman in front of the house first fired, stood a tall handsome man

59

in the prime of life, and dressed in the slightly distinctive dress of a French Protestant minister. Marie did not need Henri's whisper, "That's the minister;" and looked with eagerness at the grand, quiet face, bent down so tenderly toward his poor parishioner.

"Come home with me, Mère Agneaux," he was saying; "and let us pray the Lord to make us thankful, after all."

As they turned together, he saw the four children coming toward him, and advanced to meet them with as graceful a bow as ever Marie had seen her mother receive. Henri came forward before she could speak.

"Here is my sister, Monsieur," he said, taking Marie's hand; "and here are my two brothers."

"I am rejoiced to make the acquaintance of Mademoiselle your sister," answered the minister with another bow. And then, as Marie raised her weary face to his, with a look of childish trust and relief, he added, in a tone full of kindness: "My poor children, how tired you must be! Breakfast will be prepared in my house in a short quarter of an hour, and you should rest at once."

He led the way into his house as he spoke, Henri pointing, as he did so, to a small hole broken in one of the panes. On the threshold they were met by a lady, scarcely thirty years of age, with a sweet, happy-looking face, who exclaimed, "It is all safe, Léon; thank God, they have taken nothing. Ah, Mère Agneaux! I am so thoughtless, and you will not guess how I feel for you. You do right to come to us."

Here she paused, perceiving Marie and the boys.

"This young lady and her brothers will also honour us with their company for a time, my sister," said the minister. "This is the young gentleman who saved the village." Henri blushed as he bowed over the hand which the lady impulsively extended to him. "They have come some way, and need rest and refreshment. How soon can we have breakfast, Cécile?"

"But certainly it shall be ready directly," exclaimed Cécile, leading the way into a small, neatly furnished parlour. "Sit down, Mère Agneaux, and you too, chère Mademoiselle, and breakfast shall be here this moment, since those wretches — *tiens*, pardon me, Léon! — have at least left us our pots and pans."

By the time she had finished her speech, she had settled every one, in her kindly, energetic way: Mère Agneaux in the one easy chair, and Marie on a low chair at the window, with Louis on a footstool by her side.

"Poor little one! How tired he looks!" she continued, stooping down to stroke the golden curls from his forehead. "One moment, Léon, I want you," and the graceful little woman glided out of the room, followed by her tall brother.

She had not been gone a moment, and Marie had scarcely time to notice her surroundings — the one rare picture on the wall, the flowers in the window, and the homeliness of the furniture — when a man strode hastily in, and without appearing to see that there was any one else in the room, flung himself down on his knees by the side of Mère Agneaux, who had been quietly leaning back with closed eyes.

"O Mother, Mother!" the children heard him say, in stifled tones.

Mère Agneaux bent her gray head over him, and answered very quietly, " 'The Lord gave, and the Lord hath taken away: blessed be the name of the Lord.' "

"The *Lord!*" exclaimed the young man, starting to his feet, while his black eyes flashed with an angry light. "Do you call the king's wickedness and these brutes' work the Lord's doing!"

"Hush! hush!" answered the old woman, now thoroughly alarmed and distressed. "You must not say such things."

"I do not know why not," answered the young man moodily. He had noticed the presence of the others now, and before he could say any more, Mademoiselle Cécile came into the room, with a clean white cloth hanging over her hand, and a plate of bread, which Henri hastened to take from her. With his assistance she covered the table, and arranged plates and cups upon it from a cupboard in the room. She welcomed the newcomer to breakfast with great cordiality, and returned, after a second expedition, with a basket of hot rolls, some freshly boiled eggs, and a jar of honey. Her brother came in directly afterwards with a pot of steaming coffee and a jug of hot milk.

"You did not expect to have the rolls this morning, did you, Léon?" she asked triumphantly, as they gathered round the table. "But I had plenty of time to make them while you were out after service. I knew you would not think of breakfast till someone reminded you."

It seemed very strange to the four children to sit once more at a neatly-arranged table, bare and poverty-stricken as this one was, in comparison with their own, and they were very silent, listening to the conversation which Cécile carried on with her brother, and hearing fresh particulars of the night's alarm.

After breakfast, Cécile insisted, with authoritative kindness, that the young strangers should not only rest, but go at once to bed, and even Henri, much as he longed to be up and about, found himself quietly ushered by the minister into an upper room, where the clean sheets and pillows looked so inviting, that he and Guillaume began to think the idea was not such a bad one after all. They were asleep five minutes after they had lain down.

Marie had needed no such persuading after she had seen Louis safely disposed of, and felt that she had never really known before what a relief it was to get rid of her clothes and lie down in a bed. She did not fall asleep quite so readily as her brothers; but she slept long, and it was far on in the afternoon before she awoke. The warm golden sunlight was beginning to steal into the room; one of the windows was a little open, and she heard the voices of her two brothers down below. She lay quite still for a few moments, feeling as if she were still in a dream, and not caring to awake. Then the door was softly opened, and the kind face of her hostess looked into the room. Seeing that Marie was awake, she came to the bedside with Louis, who had evidently been washed and dressed with the greatest care, though Marie had not even missed him from his little bed at the other end of the room.

"Are you feeling better now, my dear child?" asked Mademoiselle Cécile tenderly, as she bent over Marie.

"Oh, it is such a rest!" breathed Marie out of her full heart. And then, moved to sudden confidence, she threw her arms around her new friend's neck, and kissed her.

Cécile returned the embrace with equal warmth and then assisted Marie to dress, combing out the long black hair more skilfully than Henri had been able to manage, and offering even to braid it into the fanciful erection of the period; but this Marie did not wish.

"It is so much nicer to feel it hanging loose," she said; "and Henri likes it better so. You don't think it unladylike, do you?" she added wistfully.

"No, indeed," answered Mademoiselle Lafleur warmly. "If I had my own way, no demoiselle, however noble, should wear her hair otherwise. I even like it better than the hanging plaits. Now, my child, we shall have tea very soon; will you join your brothers in the garden till then or would you prefer to remain quiet downstairs?"

"Oh, I should like to go to Henri, please," said Marie quickly.

"Come then, Mademoiselle — I do not know your name," said Mademoiselle Lafleur, who was naturally a little curious.

"Marie de St. Croix," answered the girl, her eyes filling with tears. "You know we are Protestant fugitives. It is scarce a week since our father, our mother, and Aurèle were slain in one day by such wretches as came here last night."

"My poor child!" murmured Cécile, greatly shocked.

"I cannot tell you any more just now," said Marie, trying to keep back her tears. "But, O Mademoiselle, one feels as if the good Samaritan had been sent to us. You must call me Marie."

"Indeed I will, dear Marie," answered her new friend, embracing her with almost motherly tenderness.

Downstairs they passed, along a short passage, and through a door which led to the minister's garden, and through that they went into the orchard, where the three boys were sitting under a tree. They sprung up to meet Marie with a cry of delight, and were so much engrossed with her that Cécile slipped back to her work unperceived, and left them alone.

"What a strange life ours has been lately!" said Henri, leaning back to look at the blue sky between the branches.

"Hasn't it," said Marie, with a deep sigh. "Do you know I feel as if we had been travelling, like the Arabs, through a desert and had just got to one of those oases in the middle. Shall you not be sorry to leave it again and go on in that same strange way?"

"I think it was rather a nice sort of way of living," observed Louis; "only I should like to go to bed at night; the ground is so hard to go to sleep upon."

"Poor Louis!" said Henri, patting his little brother's head. "Well, we may at least rest here one day more, Marie, for tomorrow is Sunday."

"Is it?" asked Marie eagerly. "Then that dreadful day at St. Louis-de-Linard must have been Sunday."

"Yes; we have been five days walking," assented Henri. "I wonder what sort of Sundays they have here, Marie? There does not seem to be a single Roman Catholic in the village."

"There were very few at home," answered his sister quickly. "I wonder if it is so all over France. What a strange thing it is, Henri! I never thought about it till the last week or two, and now I cannot understand why everyone should not serve God in his own religion. And it seems so strange that any one should like better to pray to the Virgin and the saints than to Jesus, or to pray in Latin instead of in French."

"Here is the minister," put in Louis, getting up from the grass and running forward to greet Monsieur Lafleur, for whom he had taken a great fancy.

"I came to see if Mademoiselle your sister was inclined for tea," said Monsieur Lafleur as he came up. "It is a little past five, and Cécile bade me tell you it was ready."

Mère Agneaux was again at tea but her son did not appear. Henri gathered from their conversation that he had already cleared out the ruins of his house, with the intention of rebuilding it as soon as possible.

After tea they went out again and sat in the garden — all but the minister, who was hard at work helping his parishioners to repair the damage done to one or two of their homes. He came back about nine o'clock, and the day closed with a frugal supper of grapes and bread, and a long, earnest prayer offered by the minister without a book.

VI

REST BY THE WAY

A long restful day followed, the happiest day that the poor children had known for weeks. It was Sunday, and the whole population assembled to worship after the Huguenot fashion in the parish church.

As they walked back to the minister's house afterwards, Henri took occasion to ask how it was that not a single Roman Catholic seemed to belong to the village.

"This parish is one of many which have professed the Reformed religion for two or three generations," replied the minister, "and the Roman Catholics have gradually died out. We have still one among us, however;" and he pointed to the chimneys of a house which stood by itself a little within the forest. "An old man lives there alone with two old servants, also Roman Catholics, and he is very bitter against the Reformed religion. I suppose we have to thank him for our pleasant surprise the other night."

"It seems a dreadful thing that such things should be done for religion," said Marie timidly. "If all of you agree, for instance, in this one village, to belong to the Reformed religion, why must you not do so? That one man could go somewhere else, surely; it seems so unjust."

"It is unjust, God knows," answered the minister earnestly. "But we are patient for God's sake; we wait His time."

"I am so tired, Marie," put in little Louis, coming to his sister's side and taking her hand. "I am so glad today is Sunday, and we have not to walk a long way!"

"He is very young for such a journey as you propose," said the minister, stooping to take the child into his powerful arms. "Do you think he can possibly manage it, my dear?"

Monsieur Lafleur and his sister knew all about their young guests now, and were full of compassion for the fate which, alas! was shared by hundreds in those troublous times.

"I cannot tell," answered Marie, with the look of womanly care which was often on her young face now. "I see nothing else to be done. I do not suppose that any letter would reach Father Gabriel safely now, and even if it did, he could do nothing for us. We can only go on, and trust in God, Henri says, and I think he must be right."

Monsieur Lafleur did not say any more now; but in the afternoon, when they had all gone for a little walk into the forest, and Cécile had gone on in front with the two younger boys, he proposed to sit down and wait for their return. They had scarcely seated themselves, when he said abruptly to Henri, "Your sister tells me that you think there is no choice for you but to go toward Bordeaux in the same fashion that you have begun."

"I know of no other," said Henri, rather surprised. "We cannot afford to go in any other way."

"And I cannot afford to send you," said the minister, sadly; "but I do not think either your sister or Louis is fit for such a journey."

"Oh, indeed, Monsieur," exclaimed Marie, "I am much stronger than I look, and have always been used to long walks."

"You should not do it if I could help it," said Henri; "but, as I said before, I do not see what else is left for us to do."

"What do you think of my plan?" asked the minister very kindly, "that you should leave your sister and Louis with us — we would do our very best for them — and that you and Guillaume should make your way to Amsterdam, and write for them when you have found your friends."

Henri turned his face downwards on the ground, and answered not a word. Marie had sprung to her feet as the minister spoke, and scarcely waited for the end of his speech to burst out with her eager protest: "O Monsieur! — no, no — a thousand times no. We might as well die at once as be separated from one another. Henri, speak! Tell him that you and I, at any rate, will never part."

"It might be our duty, you know, Marie," answered Henri in a smothered voice.

"O Henri!" she cried piteously, "I cannot bear it. First Mamma, then Papa, then Aurèle all gone, and now you! You are all I have left; I cannot part from you."

"I will leave you for a little while to think it over," said the minister, getting up. "You will, perhaps, be better able to decide by yourselves." He laid his hand upon Marie's head for an instant in passing, and heard her say as he passed out of sight, "O Henri, speak to me! Indeed I will try to do right. I will bear it, if it be God's will."

He had not gone far before he came upon his sister, also sitting down, with Louis leaning against her, and Guillaume lying in his favourite position on the grass. "They are talking it over between them," he said, in answer to a look from his sister, and then he sat down beside them, and they talked together with long pauses of delicious idleness for some time. At length Cécile declared that it was time to go back to tea, and they rose obediently to join the others. Monsieur Lafleur went on a little in advance, and soon came upon Henri and Marie.

They were sitting silently together, but Henri rose at his approach, and spoke hurriedly, "We have thought it well over, Monsieur, and though we shall ever be grateful to you for all your kindness, we think, on the whole, that we may still try to go on in the same way. Papa would have wished it if possible," he continued nervously, "and perhaps, Monsieur, there are really some reasons why it might not be a good plan. In these times you might soon be in trouble yourself — pardon me if I am wrong to say so — and there might even be a great chance of our never finding each other again. At present we can pretty well manage to go on unnoticed, and though, of course, we are tired, we are none of us really the worse for more than a week of such travelling."

"Perhaps you are right," said the minister, who had listened to Henri's speech in perfect silence. "My life is not my own, and even my sister might not always be able to remain here. It is decided, then, my dear children. May God keep you!"

"And, O Monsieur!" exclaimed Marie breathlessly, venturing to take his hand as she looked up pleadingly into his face, "you will know how we long to thank you, how grateful we really are, and how we shall ask God every night to bless you."

The minister bent down and kissed the little hand that rested so confidingly in his. "Thank you, my dear," he said; "I also will not forget you."

No one spoke of the plan again during the walk; but Cécile, when she afterwards heard from her brother of its non-success, was very much disappointed, and could scarcely be brought to see that the children might after all be in the right. She longed especially to keep little Louis but did not say anything more to Marie, as her brother seemed not to wish it. Indeed, he had good reason to know that his life was now no longer to be counted upon, and little as he thought the children fit for so long a journey, he was inclined to think that such a risk was perhaps the least of the two. Henri had written to Father Gabriel to tell him of their safety, and he had undertaken to forward the letter; but there was little chance of it ever reaching him.

At least, they did all they could to make the children's journey easier, a peasant belonging to the village willingly undertook to drive them in his cart as far as the next town, about eleven miles distant, and to direct them from there to a house where they might rest in safety for the night. Cécile slipped the greater part of her scanty store of money into Louis' pocket, with directions to give the packet to Marie the last thing at night.

It was not much past eight o'clock in the morning when the rough, springless conveyance came to the door and Cécile and her brother came out to see the children start. It was a sad parting, for they seemed to have become close friends in this little while, and there were tears in the eyes of more than one as they said goodbye.

However, none but cheerful words were spoken. They drove quickly away, and, looking back once more at the corner, they saw Cécile and her brother still standing in the sunlight with hopeful, smiling faces, and waving a last greeting as the cart turned round the corner.

VII

ON THE MARCH AGAIN

The four children had a very pleasant though somewhat silent drive to the town. Their driver was a good-natured but very ignorant man, and his accent was so bad that Henri found it difficult to understand him when he did speak. He drove them almost through the town, and drew up at a small hotel which stood on the outskirts. Here he said they could rest and dine if they chose; he should remain here for an hour or two, and before they left he would direct them on their way. However, as it was necessary for the children to spend as little as possible, and as Mademoiselle Lafleur had made up a little parcel of food which they had not yet touched, they parted from him at once, with many thanks and offers of money which he utterly refused to take.

Following the road which he pointed out to them, they soon left the town behind, and shared their simple meal in a quiet lane. It was now about one o'clock, and the sun was very hot, so that they agreed not to walk any further just yet, as less than three hours' walking would bring them to the place where they meant to spend the night. Henri fell asleep, Louis persuaded Guillaume to tell him a story, and Marie leant back against the mossy bank on which they were sitting with the intention of listening too. But her thoughts soon strayed to the happy days which seemed so long ago, and she forgot all about their present situation.

It was Guillaume who, at the end of his second story more than an hour and a half afterwards, suggested that they had better not stay too long in one place, and asked Marie if she were not rested.

71

"Oh, Guillaume, I had forgotten all about the time," answered Marie, waking out of her daydream. "Of course we ought to be going on, though it seems a shame to waken Henri."

Exactly at this moment Henri opened his eyes, and, remembering instantly their position, jumped up with the exclamation, "What! Have I been asleep? Why did you not wake me, Marie?"

"Guillaume has only just reminded me that we ought to be going on," she said. "I had forgotten all about it; but I think we have plenty of time."

They set out once more on their journey; but the day was still very oppressive, and they did not get on so fast as usual. After a time they came to a place where two roads met, and were puzzled to know which to take. One was a continuation of the lane down which they had come, and was cool and shady in comparison with the other — a straight, dusty road between two walls which led through vineyards. Marie felt sure that the driver had told them to turn off here; while the boys inclined to think that he had told them to keep to the left along the lane. As Marie found herself in a minority, she soon gave way, and they went on along the lane for a long way. It grew dreadfully rough, little more than a cart-track through waste ground thickly scattered with underwood and stunted trees.

"I think we must have come wrong after all," said Henri ruefully, as they paused for a moment and sat down to rest. "This is no regular road at all now."

"It may get better again farther on," remarked Marie, hopefully.

"I think you were right, Marie," continued her brother. "I wish we had taken the other road. I am afraid it is almost too late to turn back tonight; yet there does not seem much chance of our finding any shelter along here."

"Well, it won't be the first time we have slept on the ground," said Guillaume cheerfully. "It is hot enough for anything, and we shall easily find a safe place to sleep in."

"Well, we have still plenty of daylight left," said Henri, getting up again; "and we may get out of this wilderness again before we need think of stopping for the night. Shall we go on, Marie?"

They went on for some distance; but the road did not improve and the ground on their right rose in a steep bank to the height of a hundred feet. The children grew very tired, as they had now been walking almost continuously for nearly four hours. They were just on the point of settling to go no further, and to find a good place to sleep in, when a sudden turn in the road brought them in sight of a small log house standing quite by itself a little apart from the road. There was no sign of human habitation, and after the first exclamation of relief they began to hesitate about approaching it. It was clearly not the one to which they had been directed, and they had always been rather shy of strange houses. However, they agreed to walk round it and see what they could see before knocking at the door.

As they approached they heard a sound which at once made them forget all their doubts, and hasten forward. It was the voice of a woman calling for help, but feebly, as if she were almost exhausted. Henri ran to the door, which was unfastened, and yielded readily to his push. The voice came from the room above, and he hastily mounted the rough step-ladder, followed by the other three.

The woman was lying upon a low bedstead in a corner of the room, bound hand and foot, so that she could not move. There was no one else in the room, and as the children crowded forward to help her, the sudden relief was too much for her, and she fainted away.

Louis began to cry. Guillaume looked round for water, and seeing none, slipped downstairs again to look for some. Marie raised the poor woman's head, and Henri set instantly to work at the cords which bound her. By the time Guillaume returned with the water she had opened her eyes again, and, as her consciousness returned, she cried out in a voice of agony, "My baby! O my baby!"

The children started, and looked round; but there was no baby anywhere, and a horrible idea came into Henri's mind that perhaps the woman was mad. But she cried out again, pointing to the door into a little inner room, "The baby — my baby — it has stopped crying for the last hour! My God — if it is dead!"

Marie ran into the other room, and there, lying in a rough wooden cradle at the window, was the apparently lifeless form of an

73

infant about six months old. She bent over it with a beating heart; but before she could lift it the mother was behind her, having burst the last fastening of her bonds. She sank down on the floor as she caught her child in her arms.

There was a moment's breathless suspense while she listened. intently for the infant's breath. Marie never forgot the rapturous cry, "Alive! She is alive yet! Milk — have they left me none, then?"

Marie ran downstairs, and after a few minutes' hurried search discovered a jug half full of milk in one of the cupboards, and a cup, which she brought upstairs, and at which the poor mother snatched eagerly. At first it seemed of no use: the child was faint and drowsy, and refused all food; but after some time a spoonful of the milk was swallowed, and the child showed signs of returning life. The mother did not cease her efforts till she had disposed of quite half a cupful of milk, and a faint colour returned to the baby's cheek, when she put the milk aside and rocked the child in her arms. Then, as if she became aware of the children's presence for the first time, she looked up from her child at Marie, and said in a weary, patient voice, "Mademoiselle will think I have no manners; but I have been well-nigh driven out of my mind. The good God sent help as if by an angel; for none pass this way in general. I cannot ask Mademoiselle to sit down here; but if she and these young gentlemen will condescend to come downstairs, everything is at their service."

"Are you strong enough to move about just yet?" asked Marie kindly. "Do drink a little of this milk yourself. You must want it almost as much as the baby. Rest a few minutes longer," she continued, as the three boys stole quietly downstairs, "and then you shall come down and tell us all about it."

The poor woman leant back again with closed eyes, still, however, murmuring thanks and blessings on her unknown benefactors.

After a few minutes the baby began to cry — the sweetest sound that the world contained just then for the poor mother. She rose to her feet and walked up and down, and when it again became quiet, she invited Marie to follow her downstairs. In the room below she found the three boys, who were eager in their inquiries after the poor little baby. Nothing had been taken from the house, which was, indeed, too poor to attract even the most avaricious, and the woman hastened to set what poor food she had in store before her visitors, who were hungry enough to enjoy anything. In the course of the evening she told them that her husband had been a woodcutter, and had died about six months ago, just before the birth of his child. She had lived here very quietly ever since, subsisting chiefly on the produce of her poultry; but that morning, about seven o'clock, a small troop of horsemen had ridden up to the door and demanded food. She had nothing in the house but such poor supply of bread and milk as Mademoiselle was now kind enough to share, and they were very angry, and had called her a heretic — which indeed she could not deny, that being one reason why she still lived there by herself. Then they grew worse and worse, and only one man prevented the rest from laying hands on her. He had got them away at last, but not before they had fastened her down as Mademoiselle had just seen and there was her baby in the next room crying — crying. Ah, she prayed God that Mademoiselle might never know such a day as she had spent!

The poor woman was even more devoted to her guests when she found that they were one in faith and suffering with herself. She offered them shelter for the night before they had time to ask it, and busied herself in arranging her scanty furniture for that purpose directly after tea. They retired to rest very soon afterwards, though it was some time before sleep came to either Marie or Henri.

It was another bright day when Marie woke up the next morning, and dressing herself and Louis as quickly as possible, she sent him to see if the boys were awake, and went herself to breathe the fresh morning air outside the house.

She was struck for the first time by the beauty of this woodland home. There was a tolerably wide expanse of grass, with scanty clumps of brushwood, between the house and the steep bank — almost approaching the dignity of a cliff — which they had passed beside the night before. Behind was the forest, and single trees grew

75

pretty thickly on either side. A little to the left there was a picturesque, moss-covered shed, in front of which stood her hostess — clad in coarse, blue linen and a bright red handkerchief — throwing corn to a large flock of poultry. Marie went to meet her, and received a cheery "Good morning."

"At least, I am glad that they have not taken your hens, Madame," she said.

"There were four fine ones just ready for market," answered the widow, in a tone of regret, "and they have taken them; the rest ran into the forest. But one is thankful not to have lost more."

Marie stood and admired the pretty creatures and asked questions about them, till her brothers came running out, and the widow proposed that they should have some breakfast.

Soon afterwards they started once more on their journey, accompanied for some way by the widow, in order that they should not again miss their way. The right road was not nearly so pretty, as it led for miles through vineyards, and often the walls on either side of the road rose so high as to shut out everything from sight but the rough and endless road. It was too early yet for the gathering of the grapes, and very few people were to be met. Moreover, soon after they had entered the main road, the sky clouded over and rain began to fall, a straight, heavy downpour, from which there was no escape. They thought at first of waiting till the rain was over, but could find no shelter which would really protect them, and, besides, it seemed likely to rain for some time.

That was a dreary day. It never ceased raining, and they plodded on, wet to the skin, scarcely venturing to sit down, and only eating a hurried, uncomfortable meal in the middle of the day.

"What shall we do tonight, Henri?" asked Louis, about five o'clock, after a long silence. "We can't sleep out of doors tonight."

"No, dear, I suppose not," said Henri. "We must stay and sleep in St. Germin tonight, instead of passing through it, as we did at St. Etienne."

"Do you think we shall soon be there?" asked Louis, wistfully. "I am so tired, and the road is getting so muddy that I keep slipping."

"Poor Louis!" at once said his brothers and sister; while Guillaume and Henri offered to carry him on a "queen's cushion," and did so for some way, till he said he would rather try to walk again.

It seemed a long, long road to St. Germin, and Henri had begun to fear that they must have again missed the way, before on a little rising ground they caught sight of its lights beneath them.

By this time they were thoroughly drenched. The rain was still falling heavily, and Louis even complained that he was cold. They were glad of the gathering twilight as they passed along the damp and dimly-lighted streets, and glanced timidly at the different sign-boards. It would be the first time in their lives that any of them had slept in any sort of hotel and Marie especially looked forward to this new experience with actual dread. More than once they passed a likely-looking place, after a little consultation, without being able to make up their minds to enter.

At length, in a quiet street, they came to one where everything looked cleaner and more pleasant than those of the same grade which they had passed. The door was open, and showed two rooms — one on either side of a passage. The one on the left was, indeed, full of men smoking and drinking, but they were tolerably quiet, and through the open door of the other room they saw a stout, comely woman, sitting near the threshold, with an expression of frankness and good-humour which inclined them to approach her.

It was agreed that Henri should speak to her, and ask if they could have lodging for the night, as it was raining too heavily for them to go further.

She looked rather sharply at him for a moment, and then replied, in somewhat shrill tones, that she might perhaps have beds, but that she was not accustomed to have tramps in her house.

"But, indeed, we are not tramps," pleaded Marie, finding that Henri did not speak in answer to this charge. "We are on a journey to see some friends, and it is raining so that we do not want to go further tonight."

"But certainly it is not a fit night for such a pack of children," said the woman, not unkindly. "Haven't you got any one to look after you better than that? That poor child ought to be in bed this moment." And here she most unexpectedly took Louis up in her lap, and gave him a sounding kiss, a treatment for which Marie had to make him a hasty sign not to resent.

"I suppose, now, you've no money," was her next remark.

"Yes, we have; I think enough to pay for our lodging. And we should like some supper too, if not inconvenient to Madame," said Henri, with courtesy, which flattered the woman, though it caused her to look at him with curiosity.

"Jeanne! Jeanne," she cried out, turning toward the door. And as the summons was answered by a tall, rosy-cheeked damsel of eighteen, she continued: "Quick, then! Here are some poor, little, half-drowned wretches who want supper and lodging. They must have dry clothes first, it strikes me, unless they all want to die of a fever tomorrow. Do you take the two boys to the lads' room, and give them a drop of hot water, and any clothes of Jacques or Henri while their own are drying. I'll look after the girl and the little one."

Marie and Henri, who had with difficulty suppressed a burst of laughter at this novel description of themselves, now joined in expressing their warmest thanks to the kind-hearted woman.

"*Tiens! tiens!*" was all her remark. "Marthe Pierrot is not the woman to turn out such a set of children on a night like this." and she bustled off with Marie and Louis in such an energetic manner, that before Marie knew where she was, she found herself enveloped in dry clothes from head to foot, with Jeanne's Sunday gown (which touched the ground) upon her, and beheld Louis — looking still odder, but every inch the little gentleman that he was — in a rough sort of jersey and a pair of loose gray drawers.

Coming back into the cheerful little salon, they found Jeanne busy spreading a cloth upon the table, and when the boys came in, equally odd in their attire, Madame speedily supplied them with some excellent soup, fried eggs, and an omelette, which they all thought delicious.

During their meal she took up her knitting, and plied them with questions which they found rather difficult to answer. At last she asked Henri his name.

78

"Henri Linard," he replied, without hesitation, as they had beforehand agreed that this was a name they could honestly adopt, since all the boys had it by baptism.

"Linard!" she repeated musingly. "But yes, it is not a common name. Now, which of you might be the oldest — you or your sister?"

"We are twins," said both children, speaking at once.

"Ah, that accounts for my not being able to tell," remarked Madame Pierrot, sagely. "And how old is the little one?"

"Louis is five," said Henri.

"Poor little thing! He is not fit for such a long walk. Your mother should have known better than to send him with you.

The tears sprang to Marie's eyes as she answered, with a sob, "Our mother is dead!"

"*Tiens! tiens!*" exclaimed the woman, in vexation at her own mistake. "Poor little things! And so there is no one to look after you! One might certainly have guessed it. Well, you shall be seen to tonight, at any rate, and tomorrow you don't stir unless the weather's clear."

Jeanne, who had been serving the men in the other room, now came back again, and shortly after Jacques and Henri, merry little lads of thirteen and fourteen, came in from a visit to some neighbours. Madame Pierrot insisted on Louis going to bed, and the three older ones were thankful to follow his example. Their prayers were more fervent than ever that night, God had guided them so wonderfully. The next morning, to their great relief, was fine and clear; so, after eating an excellent breakfast, and paying a more moderate bill than they had feared, they took leave of their kind hostess with heartfelt thanks, and set out once more upon their journey.

VIII

A TERRIBLE NIGHT

It was a lovely afternoon in the end of August, rather more than a week after the events just related. In a beautiful French valley, through the middle of which ran a clear, sparkling river, its steep sides clothed with forest, four children were just sitting down to rest beneath the spreading branches of a sycamore tree.

It was a very pretty scene, and rest was very pleasant to the four De St. Croix, who had already come eight miles that day, and had to accomplish some four more before they should encamp for the night. They had grown very fond of their gypsy life, now that they were accustomed to roughing it, and, except perhaps Louis, who looked rather white and fragile, were all as strong and well as possible and able to accomplish their twelve miles a day without difficulty, even though Henri and Guillaume generally carried Louis by turns during the last two or three. The two older boys were decidedly sunburned, and Marie's colour was a little deeper than in the days of her grandeur, but her large hat had kept her complexion pretty fair.

Today was Guillaume's birthday, a very different birthday from any they had hitherto kept. Marie had thought about it all the preceding day, but when the morning came and she and Henri had met him with flattering congratulations, he had turned away, and they had not spoken of it again.

They were now talking of the prospects of their journey. The money was holding out pretty well: there were still eight gold pieces untouched, and Marie carried twelve francs in silver. There would have been more, but that two nights, besides the one they spent at St. Germin, had been too wet to sleep out of doors, and they had had to pay for lodging. However, Henri calculated that they had accomplished quite a third of their journey to the coast without spending a third of their money, and was rather inclined to forget that the French coast was not their journey's end.

"Well, I suppose we ought to be going," he said at length, getting up with a little sigh of regret.

"It is so still and pleasant just here," said Marie. "Listen! Do you hear the wood-pigeons across the valley? How pleasant it is to be in a pretty country again, after those dreary vineyards that we have been passing through lately!"

"Yes, it makes a great difference," replied her brother. "But I am afraid we must not stay here any longer now; from what we heard, it must be some way yet to Yonneville, and our path farther on, you may see, runs right into the belt of forest."

"Louis is asleep," remarked Guillaume.

"Asleep!" exclaimed Henri. "Why, it is scarcely three hours since dinner. He looks very tired, though, poor little fellow," he added, regarding the child wistfully.

"I'm afraid he ought not to walk so much," sighed Marie; "and yet I don't see how we can help it. Our money won't last unless we make at least twelve miles a day. And Louis is scarcely six years old!"

"He need not walk any more tonight, at any rate," said Guillaume. "I can carry him, and if you would slip your arm under him so, Marie, and help me to raise him, I think I can take him up without waking him."

Louis' sleep was too sound to be disturbed by their gentle movements, and they walked on at as brisk a pace as Guillaume's burden would allow. About a mile farther on they entered the forest, and found some difficulty in keeping the slightly-traced path. Louis was transferred to Henri, and, waking suddenly, was frightened at the silence and the gathering darkness of the forest. For some time the three others were entirely occupied in trying to soothe him and

81

divert his thoughts, and no one thought again about the path till Henri, choosing a moment when Guillaume was intent on Louis, whispered to Marie, "Marie, I am afraid we are going wrong. I am almost sure that we have got into a dry water-course instead of the path."

Marie gazed at him with a face of blank dismay, and, but for his instant sign of caution, might have broken out into exclamations which would have alarmed Louis still more.

"What shall we do?" she whispered at length.

"I scarcely know," was his answer. "Go on, I suppose. I don't think we have altered our course since we came into the wood, and Yonneville lies nearly straight ahead, as far as I can make out. It may prove that we have only taken a shorter and rougher way, and, at any rate, I think we should only get more hopelessly lost if we tried to find the path now, it is so dark. Don't you think so?" he added, seeing that Guillaume had listened to his last speech.

Guillaume nodded briefly, and went on talking to Louis. For some time they pressed on in the darkness, stumbling frequently, and silent with a growing sense of loneliness and fear. The wood grew thicker than ever, and at last every vestige of a path vanished, and they had to thread their way between the trees as best they could.

Suddenly Henri, who walked first, came to a standstill, exclaiming, "Hark! did you hear that?"

"I heard something," said Marie eagerly. "Listen! What can it be? — Hush, Louis darling!" — for Louis, thoroughly tired out, and startled from an uneasy doze on Henri's shoulder, was beginning to cry.

Marie's caress silenced him, and they all stood still for a few moments, listening breathlessly.

Again they heard the sound, and this time quite plainly. It was the sound of a Psalm sung by many voices at some distance in front.

A cry of relief broke from the three elder children. Though they had never attended such services with their father and mother, they had once before in the course of their journey come upon a night service held by the Huguenots, and they knew what the sound meant.

"Come on, Marie," cried Henri, springing forward, as if Louis had been but a feather's weight. "We are all right now."

Making their way through the forest in a somewhat break-neck fashion, they in a short time came so near that the words of the Psalm were distinctly audible. It was one they knew well, and with one consent they joined in the grand old song, and, so singing, they came out upon the open space where the assembly was being held.

Our gracious God has laid His firm foundations
On Zion's mount, the courts of His delight;
Her gates of splendour, bathed in heavenly light,
He loves far more than Jacob's habitations.

What glorious things, O city of God's favour,
Are spoken in melodious tones of you!
Rahab will I include, and Babel too,
With those who know Me as their LORD and Saviour.

But truly they came out upon a scene which they never afterwards forgot. The clearing was more than two acres in extent, and was one dark swaying mass of human beings. From nearly a thousand voices the sound went up of that great solemn Psalm, as from one man.

The Moor with the Philistine and the Tyrian
Shall soon, O Zion, throng your holy gate;
In songs of joy I'll hear her sons relate:
"These all were born within the walls of Zion."

God will Himself confirm it with His blessing,
And on the roll of nations He will count
All these as born on Zion's holy mount,
In many tongues one God, one faith confessing.

Then shall God's Name with holy adoration
And joyful tones be praised by Israel's throng;
Both harp and voice will blend in swelling song:
"In Zion are the founts of my salvation."

The dim light of a young moon only threw out in stronger relief the black background of the forest against a paler sky. Then, with a tremendous echoing "Amen," the song ceased; the great heaving mass swayed, as if shaken by a wind, and fell down; a thousand heads were bowed in a breathless hush waiting for prayer.

On a natural rock pulpit, in the midst of this great forest-temple, knelt a single man. Even in the dim light they could see his upturned face, radiant with the light of a great inspiration. After a moment's pause he began to pray, and in that intense living silence his every word fell clearly on the ears of the assembly. He lifted up his arms to heaven, and poured out all his fervent soul in an appeal to God.

He prayed for the country, torn and distracted with a thousand dissensions. He prayed for the Church, the "remnant of the faithful," driven out and despised of men. He prayed for the King, that he might be pardoned in this thing, and might be brought to a better mind. He prayed for all those in sorrow or in danger or in temptation at that moment, that they might be saved, comforted, and strengthened in the right way. He prayed for all those kneeling there, that they might be faithful unto death, and die in the true faith of our Lord Jesus Christ.

It was a long prayer, and when he ceased, the congregation rose with a rustle as of the leaves on a thousand trees. But the preacher remained kneeling for some moments, with his face hidden in his hands.

At length he rose, and stood, still silent, before the people, his arms hanging straight by his sides.

"How long, O Lord, how long?" The words rang out suddenly like a cry of anguish on the still night air.

"How long, O Lord, shall Thy people be trodden under foot and driven like sheep? How long shall Thine altars be desecrated with

84

a mockery of worship? How long shall the whole creation groan with travail for Thy coming, O Lord most holy — O God most mighty — O Lord God, just Ruler of heaven and earth?"

True outburst of a true heart, the flood of his eloquence swept on, and his hearers stood entranced. For more than an hour he spoke to them, pleading, exhorting, threatening, and dilating on the love of God, and the need of patient continuance in well-doing.

At length his arms fell again, and he made a pause — a long, dead pause. No one moved, and when he spoke again, his voice grew deep and almost harsh with feeling.

"I have spoken to you tonight of the many evils under which we of the true Church groan. I have exhorted you generally to patience, to steadfast faith, to courage in the cause of God. But I have somewhat still to say to you. I will speak now of one particular evil, under which not one but many of you who now listen to me are groaning in impotent despair. I will speak now of one particular thing which waits for you to do; of one particular effort of faith and courage in the cause of God which you must make tonight.

"There are things which must be borne. There are afflictions which it is the part of a good Christian to endure. We have been driven out from our churches. We have been forced to fly from our homes, and to live as the Son of man, who had not where to lay His head. We have seen our dear ones butchered before our eyes for daring to worship God in the simple and pure faith that His Son taught. We have been plundered, stripped, beaten. All this and more, even unto death, it is fit that we should bear.

"But there is one thing that we should not bear, that it is a shame and a disgrace that we should bear. I speak as to wise men; judge ye what I say. They have taken our children, the souls that God gave us to rear for His glory, and they think to bring them up in the old darkness, alien from a merciful God, conceiving hard things of Him who is our Father, hating instead of honouring the father and mother whom He has given them on earth.

"Is this a thing to be borne? Shall we who have been brought by God's mercy to a knowledge of His true light, and who have purged out the falsehood from among us — shall we sit with folded hands while *these* things are being done?

"I will speak yet more plainly. Is there one of you here tonight who does not know that within a mile of our town of Cahuzac, within scarce half a mile of the spot whereon we stand, thirty-three of our children, torn within the last three months from the bosoms of their mothers, and immured in walls both material and spiritual, are learning to love that which is an abomination unto the Lord — learning to hate the light and truth which it is our part to teach them?

"I tell you, fathers and mothers, that of you shall these thirty-three orphaned souls be required. I tell you — you who by God's grace are safe in His fold — that of you shall be required these thirty-three perishing souls. I tell you, oh my brethren, that of every one of you — yea, and of me also — will it be demanded in the last day, in the day of judgment, to give account of those thirty-three souls!"

He paused again, and the dark mass surged once more, and a low murmur arose like the storm-swell far off; but his arms were still outstretched — he had not yet finished.

"This, brethren, we must do, and that quickly. This very night must this thing be accomplished. And now I will tell you *how* it must be accomplished. There must be no violence, no plunder; not a hair of the head of these women must be harmed; all must be done decently and in order. We must do this thing and we must do it as Christian men, working in a just cause. So only, my brethren, shall this thing be acceptable unto the Lord."

His arms dropped, and, as if the tongues of all that crowd were suddenly loosened, a great clamour of confused cries shook the air, among which the only distinguishable words were: "Rescue! rescue! — to the rescue! — to the convent, the convent!"

Then he once more solemnly stretched out his arms to heaven, and the storm of sound sank and fell before him in a breathless silence. The dim light shone upon his face, and he spoke again with a voice that thrilled to the heart of the remotest listener.

"It is spoken. I charge you, all that hear me now, to follow me — in the name of the Father, and of the Son, and of the Holy Ghost."

As he ended he leaped down and pressed on through the crowd, which turned with one impulse to follow him, bursting with one accord into a stirring battle Psalm as they hurried on.

When God but speaks His mighty word,
Great is the host whose shouts are heard:
"The kings have fled like cattle!"
The women who at home abide,
Yes, even they the spoil divide,
Gained by their men in battle.
See here the wealth which they did bring:
Now silver decks a pigeon's wings
And glistening gold its feathers.
Before the LORD the kings all fled
As snow is on Mount Zalmon spread
By blasts of stormy weather.

When the four children had first come upon the ground, many of the outsiders, who saw that they were strangers, had with ready courtesy moved aside to let them pass on, so that by the time the service ended they were in the thick of the crowd, and were obliged to follow its movement even had they not wished it. It was very difficult for them, and especially for Guillaume, who had now charge of Louis, to keep up with the swift marching pace of the congregation; but in the darkness they had no choice but to stumble on breathlessly, sheer desperation alone enabling them to do so.

Marie felt as if she were moving on in an endless dream. The swift movement through interminable forest trees, the darkness, the tramp of a thousand feet around her, and the singing of a thousand voices in that echoing Psalm, seemed almost too bewildering to be real. She could only cling tremblingly to Henri's hand, and follow with the rest as fast as her feet could carry her.

Once Henri paused for one moment to take Louis from his brother, and even in that moment the pressure was so great that Marie fell, and Guillaume dragged her up and on almost by main force. After what seemed hours to Marie, but was really not half an hour, the forest thinned and fell away, and they passed into a small open valley. Here there was no sign of human habitation, except one great block of buildings standing near the opposite edge of the forest; evidently the convent which was their object.

Still singing the Psalm, which they had only finished to begin again, the great human wave swept across the half-reaped field, and surged round the high dark walls. One or two lights flitted hastily from one part of the building to another, but there was no sound at their approach.

> *With mighty chariotry untold,*
> *His host ten thousand thousandfold,*
> *The LORD came to His nation.*
> *From Sinai's mount He made His way*
> *To Zion, which He made for aye*
> *His Holy habitation.*
> *Thou didst, O LORD, ascend again,*
> *With many captives in Thy train*
> *And gifts from men obtaining,*
> *From even those who did rebel,*
> *That here the LORD our God may dwell,*
> *Here evermore remaining.*

The Psalm of the besiegers ended, and Marie found herself pressed back again with her brother by the crowd, who were evidently being arrayed in something like order, a short distance from the walls, by the preacher, whose voice they could hear above all the rest, though they could not yet distinguish what he said.

At length he managed to restore silence, and they made out that he, in company with one or two more, advanced to the great door of the convent, and knocked and rang in due form. After a time a grated aperture in the door was opened, and a face appeared, at the sight of which even the murmur of the crowd was silenced utterly, that all might hear what she had to say.

Even then her speech was inaudible to those who were not in the front rank, but the preacher's voice rang out clearly in answer, "We wish to speak with the lady abbess, to demand from her the immediate surrender of the thirty-three children of the Reformed religion unlawfully detained within these walls."

An answer was returned almost immediately, to the effect that the lady abbess gave audience to no person at that hour of the night, and must request the gentleman who spoke immediately to withdraw with his followers.

An angry clamour rose from the expectant crowd, silenced at once by a gesture from the preacher.

"Tell the lady abbess," he answered boldly, "that we regret to cause her any inconvenience, but that we refuse to leave this spot until our children are delivered up to us."

With little delay they received for answer that the abbess knew nothing of any children of the Reformed religion; that there were some children in the convent, but that, by the blessing of Our Lady, they were all good Catholics.

A storm of execration burst from the crowd, when they understood this answer, beyond the power of the preacher to silence. Threats, groans, and shouts for the lady abbess continued without intermission, till Marie wondered when it would end.

She found a comfortable and safe resting-place in the arm of a splendid tree for Louis, and stood by his side ready to take him in her arms again should there prove the least occasion. Henri and Guillaume grew tremendously excited, though they still remained by their sister instead of pressing to the front.

The outcry grew frightful, and some of the rougher of the mob even began to throw stones at the windows, giving unmistakable hints that they would not be restrained much longer. At this juncture word was passed along the crowd that the abbess was coming to the balcony to speak with them, and the riotous members were brought back to order.

In a few moments a long narrow window which led on to a small stone balcony just above the great door was opened, and a tall, stately figure appeared, quite alone. A few of the foremost in rank had contrived to possess themselves of torches of some sort, and in the red, fitful light she was plainly seen. Her dress was long, white, and flowing; a peculiar black head-dress passed round her face, and descended some way upon her shoulders. Her face was not clearly visible, but the clear firm tones which rang out through the silence which followed her appearance showed plainly what sort of expression it wore.

"I am told, messieurs, that you desire to speak with me. You come in a strange manner, and at a strange time; yet I am ready to hear what you have to say, and request you to prefer your business with speed."

She was answered by tumultuous cries of "The children! — the children! Give us back the children!"

As soon as the noise subsided, she answered coldly, "I can hold no parley with a confused rabble. If there *be* a leader among you" — and the contemptuous accent was not lost upon the crowd — "let him stand forth and answer me with the best grace and fewest words at his command."

The preacher at once advanced in front of his followers, and bowing with extreme courtesy to the proud figure above him, made answer at once, "Madame, we come to demand the instant surrender of thirty-three children of the Reformed religion received by you from the king's officers during the last three months, and now within these walls."

There was a moment's pause, and then the clear tones answered, with the same proud scorn, "You do well and bravely, messieurs, to come thus at dead of night and think to frighten a handful of women into compliance with your unlawful and insolent demands. The children of whom you speak are well and happy; they are fast throwing off the poisonous influence which blighted their young lives and desire nothing less than a return to their errors. And I, who have saved them from worse than death, from the very jaws of Satan, think you that I will yield them back again? I tell you that rather will every one of us die this night, and thus present ourselves unstained before our Maker, with the souls which we have won for Him."

90

Again there was a pause, and an undecided murmur among the crowd, on whom the accusation of cowardice in their mode of proceeding had made a momentary impression.

At that moment the window behind the tall motionless figure on the balcony was pushed violently open, and in an instant a slight girlish figure in white, with a cloud of wild hair streaming behind her, stood on the extreme edge of the stone parapet.

There was a sudden awe-struck hush at the sight of this apparition, and then a shrill childish voice penetrated even to the outskirts of the crowd.

"It is a lie that she has told you. We are all true, even unto death. If ye be men, if ye be indeed followers of the true religion, save us now, before it be too late."

She got no further, for strong hands were laid upon her from behind, and she was borne struggling back into the convent. But she had done her work. With one tremendous shout, "God to the rescue!" the whole mass of the people flung itself, like one great wave, upon the convent walls.

The sudden movement left the De St. Croix children alone, some way behind the hindmost of the besiegers.

"Oh, Marie!" cried Henri and Guillaume in one breath, "it is impossible to stay. Are you not safe here with Louis?"

"Go, in God's name," answered Marie simply, but with a noble flash in her dark eyes; "I will pray for you."

The two boys needed no second bidding before dashing into the thickest of the crowd. Marie, bending to see if Louis were frightened, discovered that in the midst of all the uproar he had fallen fast asleep. She thought with compassion how very tired he must be, and wrapping closer around him the blanket which they had carried all through their journey, she stood waiting for the end of this terrible night.

The shouts and cries seemed to increase every moment. Some of the crowd had been detached so as to surround the building, yet in many places there was only a thin line of guard; but all were hammering at the doors and windows — even, with an insane frenzy, at the very walls. Marie tried to pray but her brains seemed spellbound; she could only gaze with a species of fascination at the scene before her.

Suddenly a still louder cry of mingled horror and exultation rose from the crowd, and looking toward the spot, she beheld flames rising from behind a lower part of the wall. A lighted torch flung frantically over the wall by some one more reckless than the rest had fallen upon the roof of some small outbuildings, and the light wind caused the flames to gain ground with fearful rapidity.

Up to this moment the inmates of the convent had remained perfectly silent and invisible since the retreat of the abbess; but now wild shrieks were heard as the fire became plainly visible, and seemed to envelop almost all the lower stories of the convent. The besiegers called loudly to the women to come out, and battered at the great door more furiously than ever, maddened by the shouts of the women among the crowd, who cried out that the children would perish in the flames while they knocked idly at the door.

It was a terrible sight — the great dark forest hemming in the scene on every side — the dark, surging mass of human beings, that beat like water against those black, immovable walls, which rose high above them, girt about the middle with a wreath of spreading flames. How those flames danced and writhed like fiery serpents, throwing a red lurid light over everything, ringing a crimson blush even over the face of the still, starlit heaven. And Marie stood apart; with one arm supporting her sleeping brother on the old tree stump, her face white and still, her beautiful eyes flashing, her body motionless, but her whole heart throbbing with one wild, inarticulate prayer to God.

Suddenly, as she gazed, a long narrow window near the roof of the convent, above the flames, was flung open, and there stood, it seemed upon the sill, the same apparition they had seen before — the slender white figure, with the cloud of streaming hair, thrown out into strong relief by the lurid sea of flame beneath. A cry broke from the crowd at the sight of her, but she waved her hand, and great silence fell upon them.

"Get up to the little balcony," cried the shrill young voice, making itself heard above the roar and crackle of the flames. "I cannot come down, but all the rest are together in that room. You will save them if you do not lose a moment."

"Come down!" shouted up the thousand voices to her as one man "Come down, or you are lost!"

"I cannot," she answered. "Bear me witness that I died in the faith of my race, and made an end worthy of my fathers. For Christ's sake hasten, or they will all be lost."

Even as she spoke, the window below was opened, and a crowd of nuns rushed out upon the balcony.

But the abbess was in front of them, and, standing on the very spot from which she had dragged back the girl, turned round and confronted the frightened, trembling women. "Back! back!" they heard her cry. "Cowards! Have ye not vowed to die a martyr's death?"

At this moment one of the nuns stooped and threw a rope over the edge of the balcony. The abbess saw it, and tried in vain to prevent it, but they were too quick for her, and eager hands below caught and held it fast.

"Take her away! Take her away!" cried the nuns. "The children are all here, and we would let them down, but she will let no one pass."

Before the words were finished, a young agile fellow of twenty, much above the ordinary height of Frenchmen, climbed up the rope, and stood by the side of the abbess.

"Permit me, Madame," he said, and the next instant he had taken up the tall dignified woman, as easily as if she had been a child, and dropped her over the parapet, so that she was obliged to slide down the rope. The rest would have followed instantly, but the young man waved them back. "Bring out the children" he said sternly, and one by one the poor frightened little things, many of whom had nothing on but their night-clothes, were passed through from the room within, and went safely down the rope, to be cried over, and blessed, and welcomed by the crowd below.

"Are the thirty-three there?" shouted the young man, as the last was lowered.

"All safe," was the answer.

"Pass then, Mademoiselle," he said, offering his hand to the foremost nun who was not slow to avail herself of the permission.

As the man, last of all, slid down the rope, a long wild cry from above turned all eyes upwards again to that slender white figure, standing now with red flames almost at her feet, and a background of starlit sky seen through the window; for part of the back-wall had already fallen in.

At the sound the abbess, who had been standing aside mute and motionless, looked up and saw the girl.

"Holy Mother!" she exclaimed in horror, "let me go back that I may die with her."

She actually attempted to ascend the rope in order to re-enter the burning room, but strong hands held her back, and voices in the crowd cried out, "Look, look, she is gone!"

The figure above had disappeared. Every face of the thousand was upturned, and for several minutes there was an awful, intense silence. And then with a roar and crash, which shook the very ground beneath their feet, the whole of the top of the building fell in.

Louis woke with a scream of fright. "Guillaume! Guillaume!" he cried; but Marie could not cry for Henri. Her tongue clove to the roof of her mouth. Instinctively she caressed Louis, while her eyes, dilated with horror, were fastened upon the dreadful scene, looking only for that which she did not see — some trace of her brothers.

The awe-struck crowd silently withdrew from those crushed and burning ruins, bearing more than one who had been struck by the falling stones. The nuns formed in a small procession, and took their way toward the distant town, singing a *Dies Iræ*. The gray light of dawn began to steal over the ghastly scene. Full twenty minutes must have passed, and still Marie stood motionless, with one arm round her little brother, and wild fixed eyes.

Suddenly Louis cried again, "Guillaume! Guillaume!" and this time he was answered by a shout, as three figures came running from behind the ruins, and Marie fell on her knees in wordless thankfulness, feeling rather than seeing that her prayer was granted. The next moment she was clasped in Henri's arms, while Louis flung himself recklessly from his perch upon Guillaume, and then Marie cried out almost in fear, for in the third figure, clad in white serge, with streaming hair and uncovered head she recognized the young girl who had seemed to perish before their eyes.

"You are safe, then!" she exclaimed in astonishment, as the new-comer threw herself into Marie's arms.

"Safe and unhurt, thanks to God and to your brothers," answered the clear, ringing tones which had made themselves heard to such good purpose that night. "But what nobleness! what devotion!"

"You saved her?" asked Marie, turning to her brothers in still greater astonishment, and then, perceiving that Guillaume's head was tied round with his handkerchief, she added in terror, "O Guillaume! How is this — you are hurt."

"It is but a trifle," answered Guillaume, who was very pale, but as quiet as ever. "Come away, Marie; let us rest out of sight of this."

They went into the wood a little way, and sat down on the soft fragrant moss to discuss their adventures.

"I do not quite understand how you came to be in the convent," said Marie to the new-comer, after a little while. "There were thirty-three counted out besides you."

"I was never one of thirty-three, nor do I belong to the people," replied the young lady, with a slight accent of hauteur. "I am Léonore Isabelle Virginie Felicité, Comtesse de Villeneuve, and head of my race."

"But you are of the religion?" asked Marie anxiously.

"I am of the religion of my father, and he was a Protestant. Do you want to know how I came into the convent? Because my father refused to sign the Abjuration, they quartered the dragoons upon us; because we tried to escape, they hunted him and shot him down; because I was wealthy, and no son, they spared my life, and would have married me to my cousin, who is as good a Roman Catholic as he is a bad man, and who is twice as old as I am to boot; because I rebelled, and sang my father's Psalms, without looking at the count whenever he came to see me, they confiscated all my property, and

95

sent me to the convent. Ah! But I led them a life," continued this strange girl, not perceiving that her listeners looked somewhat astonished as she went on. "I flung the Virgin from the altar, I said my own prayers out loud when they were at mass, I dropped a spider into the holy water when the abbess was going to cross herself; there is no end to the tricks we played upon each other. They took all clothes from me but the habit of a novice, and I unstrung the rosary they gave me, and made bracelets out of it. They used to have a fight with me to cut my hair, and I flung it into their eyes, and then jumped on to the window sill, and made as if I would throw myself out when they came near me. Yesterday I was fourteen, and the abbess had determined that my hair should be left no longer. They came behind me by stealth, and pulled my hair all down; but I was too quick for them. Oh, what a chase I gave them all that day!" and she shook back the hardly kept hair with laughing pride in the recollection.

"And how did you get free of them at last?" asked Marie with eager interest.

"Oh, I got into the abbess' own cell, while they were chasing me over the convent, and barricaded the door against her," answered the girl with a burst of laughter, "and exchanged compliments through the keyhole. They got tired at last, and went away. But they came back again, to console me with the amiable announcement that I should not have a morsel of food till I came out and submitted, and just as I was assuring the abbess that I was perfectly ready to starve in her chamber, and haunt her every night afterwards, I heard a sort of little scuffle in the convent, and then everybody ran away at once. I thought it was a ruse at first and waited till I heard the noise of a great crowd outside; then I guessed what had happened, and stole out very cautiously. I got into the great room without anyone seeing me, and then I made a rush for the window, as you saw."

"Yes; you did that well," said Marie admiringly. "But what did the abbess do to you?"

"Oh, we fought each other all the way up to that little room, and then she managed to push me in and lock the door."

"Then how was it you were saved?" asked Marie with a shudder.

Léonore's ready flow of words was silenced as she held out her hand to Henri, and the quick tears sprang to her eyes. "I believe he came through the fire," she said in a low tone.

"It was Guillaume's doing," said Henri briefly. "He found the rope, and he was waiting on the cloister roof to hold it fast as we came down."

"What! You slid down a rope outside!" exclaimed Marie in horror. "How could you manage it?"

"I shall never know to my dying day how we managed it," answered Léonore in a tone of deep feeling. "But we came down somehow — see my hands" — and Marie had a momentary glimpse of palms scratched and bleeding from the friction of the rope — "and they seized and dragged me to the very end of the cloister roof, just in time."

"Yes; the convent fell sooner than I thought it would," continued Henri, as Léonore broke off and shuddered. "The shock threw us down almost senseless for some minutes, and the stones rattled like great hail all round us, but only a little one hit Guillaume and when, after a while, we looked about us for the best way to get down, we found that the *débris* made it much easier."

"Oh, if I had known," gasped Marie, covering her face with her hands.

Henri put his arm tenderly around her. "Hush, my Marie," he whispered; "your prayers helped to save us, and it is all over now."

"Yes, it is all over now," exclaimed Léonore, recovering her spirits as suddenly as she had lost them. "Let us be reasonable, and consider what is next to be done. You — do you belong to any place about here? I can see you are not of the people."

"Oh, no," said Marie sadly; "we are noble, but we are orphans and outcasts like you, and are now on our way to Bordeaux, intending to sail from there to Amsterdam."

"What a capital idea!" exclaimed Léonore with enthusiasm. "You will let me join your party, won't you? For France is now hateful to me."

97

"Oh, yes; you shall come with us," answered Marie and the two elder boys together, while Louis looked at Léonore with puzzled eyes, as if he did not quite understand the arrangement.

Guillaume here interposed with a suggestion that they should take some rest, as none of them except Louis had slept that night. The three others scouted the notion of sleepiness; but as they did not wish to proceed just yet to the village, they agreed to rest a while in the same place, and Guillaume's eyes twinkled with lazy satisfaction as he saw them gradually fall asleep around him before he followed their example.

IX

THE DESERTED VILLAGE

It was nearly noon when Marie opened her eyes, and at first she did not remember anything that had passed during the night.

However, as she lay still in those few delicious moments which come on first waking, her eyes fell upon the young countess, who had evidently been awake some time, and had paid a visit to the little stream which ran near them, she looked so fresh and bright. Marie lay still, and did not speak, in order that she might observe this new friend at her leisure.

Léonore, Comtesse de Villeneuve, looked more than the fourteen years which she had completed yesterday. She was tall and slight — taller even than Marie — with a little head, and tolerably good features. In fact, she would have been very pretty but for her complexion, which was so dark as to give an almost uncanny effect to her large, brilliant, blue eyes, and a mass of tawny hair which came down to her waist, and much resembled a lion's mane. She was leaning back against the stem of a pine tree, apparently listening to the cooing of a pair of doves which were somewhere out of sight.

At length Marie sat up, and said softly, "Léonore."

Léonore turned round with a start and a look so like anger that Marie shrunk a little, and seeing this, the other laughed somewhat uneasily, and said, "Pardon, Mademoiselle; but the truth is, I have been so little accustomed to hear myself addressed by my Christian name, that for the moment it took me by surprise."

"It is I who should ask pardon, Mademoiselle le Comtesse," answered Marie gently, but with a little flush on her cheek. "I did not mean to take a liberty."

With a quick change of mood, which Marie soon learned to look for in this strange girl, Léonore flung herself down by Marie's side, and buried her face in the folds of Marie's dress.

"Oh, call me Léonore!" she cried out with a stifled sob. "I am so tired of my rank and my loneliness, and I can bear my father's name from you. Let us be sisters, since neither of us has another."

Marie embraced her with all her old impetuous warmth, and the first scene of what promised to be lasting friendship was only ended by the waking of three hungry boys, who, though they cast sympathetic glances at the tell-tale face of their guest, were urgent in demanding that they should at once begin the day's walk, and procure some breakfast at the nearest village.

They set out accordingly, and made the best of their way through the now silent valley, passing by the ghastly ruins of last night's work with averted looks, and the low-toned question which each had as yet feared to ask the other — whether any one had been killed.

Marie thought not. She knew one or two of the people had been hurt by the falling of the wall, but did not think any one had been crushed or burnt. As they came out into the cultivated country again, they expected to meet someone of whom they could ask news; but the whole land seemed deserted.

"Here is a village!" exclaimed Henri, as they reached the top of a vineyard slope; "now we shall at least get something to eat."

"I see nothing stirring," said Marie, shading her eyes to look down; "there is not even a dog or a goat to be seen anywhere. It is getting quite dreadful, Henri. I feel as if we had got into an enchanted land."

They went on rather silently along the dusty road, but still they met no one. When they entered into the village, the street was silent and deserted, and when they knocked at the doors, the houses echoed emptiness.

"The whole village seems to have gone away," said Henri, coming back to them after another vain trial, "and yet all the doors that I have tried are fastened. I suppose there is nothing for it but to walk on."

They went further down the street, and turning a corner came upon a broad open space, evidently the village market-place, in the centre of which was a stone fountain, with rude stone seats in four angular recesses. On one of these sat an old woman, quietly knitting in the noonday sun, with one or two pigeons making circles against the unclouded blue sky overhead, and two sitting near her on the fountain brim.

"Here is something alive at last!" cried Léonore, as she ran forward to the old woman, who did not look up until she came quite close, nor rise even then — a lack of respect which it was evident so disconcerted Léonore that she stood hesitating until the others came up.

"*Bonjour*, Madame," began Henri, lifting his hat with the ready courtesy of a gentleman. "Could you tell us where we may obtain food with the least delay?"

The old woman regarded them all for some moments, and then answered as if talking to herself, "Well, well; one knew the world must turn topsy-turvy; but it might have stayed there, and not continue to turn somersaults like a Paris *gamin*. Food, said you? Yes, yes: one day the heretics, the next day a priest; a beggar riding in the morning, and a noble begging in the afternoon."

"We are not beggars!" broke out Léonore, angrily. "*Tenez donc!* Do you not see that we who speak to you are noble?"

"Pardon, Madame," said Marie, pressing gently to the old woman's side before she could answer; "we are able to pay, and only want to know where we may find some auberge or baker's in this place."

"You will find no one to wait on you today, my pretty lady," answered the old woman, in a softer tone. "The whole village has gone into hiding for fear of dragoon justice. Do you not know what they did last night, the villains?"

"Did they burn the convent?" asked Marie, in a faltering tone.

"Helped to do it," answered the old dame; "and came back like a whirlwind at six o'clock this morning, with the holy women trudging in the midst. Ah well, poor things, they are heretics, and deserve all, else it were a glad sight to see those poor women with their babes again — only, when one thinks of their souls!"

"What became of the nuns?" asked Guillaume, earnestly.

"Gone to the House of Mercy at Cahuzac," was the reply. "Most of our Catholics went with them to escort them, threatening to inform; so there was soon a panic among the heretics. They went off with the thirty-three children into hiding, and every soul left in the village trembled and went also. The place is ready for the dragoons, you see."

"And you, good mother, what will you do?" asked Henri.

"I!" answered the old woman, with a proud lifting of her hoary head; "I have not set foot out of the village for twenty years. I am a good Catholic, and fear nothing." She had scarcely ceased knitting all this time, and now went on silently as if she had forgotten their presence.

"I suppose we must go on further," said Marie, with a sigh. "Good mother, can you tell us how far it is to the next village? We have had no breakfast yet."

"What! And it is now dinner-time," said the old dame, looking up with more interest. "Ah well, I can manage something for you if Mademoiselle and her brothers and sister will enter my poor dwelling yonder."

She was answered with earnest thanks, especially from the boys, who had not at all relished the idea of a further walk before eating, and in a short time they were doing justice to a plain but excellent breakfast which the old woman spread for them. She was delighted with the moderate payment which Marie slipped into her hand before departing, showered down blessings from all the saints upon them, and embraced Louis fervently. They left her sitting in her old place by the sunny fountain, with the pigeons for her sole companions.

"Marie," burst forth Louis indignantly, as soon as they were out of hearing, "why do all the old women want to kiss me since we left St. Croix?" His brothers and sister laughed, and Léonore exclaimed, "Well said, little one! Noble blood does not like such familiarity. I would not allow it if I were you."

"I don't know how to help it," answered the child petulantly. "They would not like it if I refused; but they used not to be so rude."

"Well, Darling," answered Marie, who had found her gravity again, after Léonore's silly speech, "it is just because they would not like it if you refused that you must try not to mind it now and then, because, you know, they mean to be kind, and it would never do for a De St. Croix to be rude."

Louis still could not make out why it should be, and it took some time for his brothers to console him under these repeated affronts to his dignity. However, the beauty of their walk soon dispelled all grievances, and the five children pressed merrily on, passing by Cahuzac about five o'clock — for they always avoided entering towns when possible — and eventually found shelter for the night in a small auberge four miles farther on.

X

THE LEGEND OF FIERCE FULK IRONHEART

After this incident in their journey, a new interest and a new care entered into Marie's life — or rather into the twins' lives; for the strong affection between Marie and Henri had only been deepened by their joint suffering and responsibility, and neither had a thought or an anxiety unshared by the other.

The new interest was, of course, Léonore. She was a constant subject of wonder or amusement. Her violent party-feeling shocked the De St. Croix children, who had been brought up in very different principles, and could not understand how a Protestant could bear such intense hatred to all Roman Catholics as she seemed to do. If they passed a crucifix, she would rail at it for a graven image, and even fling stones in the hope of breaking it, until she saw that this really distressed them. She declaimed violently against the King, the Pope, and all the saints in the same breath, and laughed away all attempts at anything like argument.

Guillaume, though as quiet as ever, had wakened into actual animation under the influence of the friendship which the capricious young countess bestowed chiefly upon him. The two were always together, often a little in advance of the other three, and both being excellent walkers, they made extra little excursions whenever the wayside was particularly beautiful. Often, when it was drawing near the time for their midday meal, the three others would come suddenly upon Guillaume and Léonore whom they had lost sight of for a short time, and would find their dinner daintily spread out and sheltered from the sun; while Léonore would be lying full length in the most comfortable nook, and Guillaume fanning her with a great green branch.

She possessed a lovely voice, too, clear, fresh, and strong, and as a De St. Croix it was necessarily to be a singer — though since their troubles the four children had scarcely had the heart to sing — Léonore had not been two days with them before she discovered their neglected talent, and gave them no rest till they had sung her all their songs and learned many of hers. They used to march along the road singing Marot's Psalms for an hour together, and then, with a merry laugh, Léonore would break away suddenly, calling Guillaume to follow her. She had a passion for flowers, and at every resting place wove fresh ones into her hat and hair, which she wore loose like Marie.

Then after supper, when they "camped" for the night, they fell into a habit of singing together, either in part or in unison, for a lengthened half-hour — "our evening concert" they grew to call it. And in after-days perhaps no part of that memorable journey was remembered by them with such regretful affection as those evening concerts, when the day's journey was over, and they leaned back at their ease in the starry summer twilight, often without a fire in that warm, fragrant air, and sang together the stirring Psalms of the Reformed. Sometimes, if Léonore, in her changeful moods, was disinclined to sing, they ceased after the first two or three songs, and Guillaume spun out his marvellous tales, as much to Léonore's satisfaction as the rest. Or at another time, Léonore, who had been well taught and knew a number of exquisite songs, would begin alone, and hold the others, children though they still were, entranced by the beauty of her voice and words.

One evening she was unusually silent, and lay back on the grass, refusing to allow that she was tired, but scarcely joining at all in the songs which they commenced as usual. It was a lovely night — warm and clear, with a bright moon. The five children were sitting in a little sheltered hollow, aside from the road, which here ran through a chain of low, uncultivated hills. They had not walked quite so far as usual that day, as, being short of food, and seeing no signs of human habitation they had stopped to fish for at least an hour before sunset. Then Léonore had been in her blithest mood, and while Henri cleaned the fish, she and Guillaume had collected plenty of dead wood for a fire, and had found this nook to sleep in. Since tea, however, she had spoken little, and even repulsed Guillaume when he would have moved some dry grass to place her head more comfortably.

"Why do you stop?" she asked, as, finding that she did not join, they did not begin a fresh song.

"What would you like to sing, Léonore?" asked Henri gently.

She was silent for a moment, and then said, in a tone so soft and gentle that it scarcely seemed to belong to Léonore: "I do not know how it is; my heart is full of song, and yet I cannot sing with you tonight. I am thinking — thinking of a song that I used to sing in the old days; a song of the De Villeneuves, and a prophecy."

"Sing it to us now, dear Léonore," said Marie.

"I do not know if I can," answered Léonore, and there was again silence for some moments.

Then she sat up suddenly, half kneeling, with the moonlight on her tawny hair and in her strange, brilliant eyes; a look also on her face which they had never seen before. She began to sing; began in a low, sweet voice, which gradually rose to its full power, or sunk wailingly, as the song went on. It was a kind of legend that she sang — the story of a black deed done by one of the early ancestors of the Villeneuve race: — how Fulk de Villeneuve, a fierce man and mighty in war, married a fair young wife, who trembled and wept on her wedding day. How, after that she had borne him a son, Satan found means to kindle dark and unjust suspicions in the breast of Fulk Ironheart. How that he had made a great feast in his castle, and had bidden his fair young wife robe herself right royally to do him honour. How he had caused a great stake to be planted, ere the morning of the fête should dawn, before the castle windows, and how one watching had seen dark forms flit to and fro the whole night piling fagots round it. How, when the day was brightest, and the people thronged to the feast, there were laid out great tables groaning with good cheer, and the red wine flowed like water, and there were music and great merry-making, and how, when the feast was over, and the people waited, fierce Fulk Ironheart rose up before them all, and taking his fair wife's hand, they went in a grand procession out from the castle to the stake. How the dark, shrouded figures — devils were they all — had appeared then from the pile, and had taken and bound that fair lady in the sight of all the people. How the flames rose up fiercely around her, and all the people wept and cried to Fulk Ironheart to save her, though none stirred to do so from terror of his name. How he laughed as he strode back into the castle, and bade the soldiers strike up some sparkling music for the dance. How the heavens grew dark and muttered, as the people went away lamenting for the death of that fair lady. How all that night long the babe wept sore, and would not be comforted. How, in the pale dawn of the morning, when only the nurse watched by the wailing babe, there stood by his cradle, suddenly and without sound, a tall white figure, and the nurse knew it for the figure of her dead lady, and she bent over the babe, and signed his brow with the sign of the cross, and his wailing was stilled. How the nurse heard her speak strange words, and knew that she laid a curse upon the house of De Villeneuve — that every wife of their race should die before her time; that one in every generation should perish by a violent death; until, in the fifth century, the race should end in a woman, and perish out of the land. How, when she had finished speaking, she bent down to kiss the babe, and he fell asleep with a smile on his face; but she faded away as the sunlight touched her, and was never seen again.

The long twilight deepened into night — the fire burned low — and still Léonore knelt and sang, sang with a voice which went out far into the night, or sunk with a wail more sweet and sorrowful than they had ever heard before. All listened in a breathless hush, till the exquisite notes quivered with an undertone of horror at the close of the song. Then no one moved or spoke, till Léonore, who at the last faltering word had bowed down her face till it was hidden on her knees, suddenly sprung up, exclaiming, in her usual clear, decided tones, "Pardon, *mes amis!* I did not intend to sing you such a doleful rhyme. I do not know what moved me so." And then, with a little nervous laugh, she went out of the hollow in the moonlight, and left them.

Guillaume sprung up, and ran to the entrance of the hollow, where he paused, evidently keeping Léonore in sight, but hesitating whether to follow her. Marie turned her beautiful eyes to Henri, so full of a vague awe and horror that it helped him to conquer the strange, eerie feeling with which Léonore's song had led him.

"Marie, dear Marie," he said quickly. "Don't look like that! It was only a strange old legend that she sang; nothing that any one need care for now."

"If it should be a prophecy!" gasped Marie. "It is the fifth century."

"Don't let it trouble you, *chère petite sœur*," answered her brother, tenderly; "it does not often trouble Léonore, you see. All happens as God wills, not according to the legendary curse of some poor wronged woman."

"It may be so," sighed Marie; "but I am glad we have no De St. Croix legend so terrible. Where do you think Léonore has gone, Henri?"

"She is all right," said Henri, who was much more concerned for his sister than for the last Countess of Villeneuve. "Guillaume will not lose sight of her, and she will be back to go to bed directly, as we should all have done before this. Louis has been sound asleep for some time."

"Yes, but it is not like Louis to fall asleep while the singing is going on," said Marie, her attention instantly diverted, as Henri meant it should be, when she looked down at the little fellow lying like a fair waxen figure at her side, with the moonlight on his white face and golden curls. "He looks very tired. Don't you think so, Henri?" she added wistfully.

"Oh no, Marie. It is only that you are tired, and ready to fancy all sorts of dreadful things tonight," answered Henri, with a cheerfulness which he could ill feign; for he had been very anxious about Louis for some days past, only he did not wish Marie to dwell upon it tonight. "Come, Darling," he went on coaxingly, "give me the brush, and let me begin to do your hair. Léonore will be back directly, and want to go to sleep at once."

He had scarcely spoken, when Léonore and Guillaume came back together, laughing and talking as if they had been doing nothing else all the evening.

"Ah, you have begun already!" exclaimed Léonore, throwing herself down on the bank. "Come, Guillaume, make haste, we are dreadfully late."

Guillaume obediently took the brush which his sister handed to him, and set to work on Léonore's mass of hair, which was always far more tangled than Marie's. But ever since the first night, when she had seen Henri acting tire-woman to his sister, this imperious young countess had claimed the like service from Guillaume, and as he had never by look or gesture expressed the smallest disinclination, it grew to be considered by all of them as a mere matter of course. It was not long after that before they lay down to rest, and, in spite of all that might have troubled them, slept the sound sleep of tired, healthy youth.

XI
TROUBLES THICKEN

Marie's first waking thought the next morning was of Louis. His evident unfitness for their mode of travelling and his increasing delicacy were now her greatest care, and though she and Henri never spoke about it, each knew and shared the other's fears. He had grown much thinner since they left St. Louis-de-Linard, and his great blue eyes shone with an unnatural light in his pale face. He scarcely ever complained; but his merry laughing ways were all gone, and instead he was learning an intelligence and a comprehension of their position which was almost painful to the two elder ones.

Guillaume, once inseparable from his little brother, had scarcely seemed to notice it, and he was now so frequently in front with Léonore that the task of carrying Louis when he grew tired devolved much more frequently upon Henri. Louis did not seem to notice the defection of his favourite brother, except that now and then Marie saw a wistful look when Guillaume disappeared, and he once or twice asked his brother to stay and tell him a story instead; nor did he ever ask in vain. Besides, sometimes the two would take Louis with them, and the delight of riding on Guillaume's back, while Léonore walked laughing and singing beside them, almost made up for Guillaume's forgetfulness at other times.

On the morning after that night when Léonore sang the legend of the Fair Wife of Fierce Fulk Ironheart, Henri awoke, as usual, before the others, and crept to Marie's side to look at his little brother. He still slept, but his breathing was not so regular as it should have been; his dry lips were slightly parted, and there was a flush upon his cheek that even Henri knew was not the bloom of health. The two girls lay in the same place, side by side — a curious contrast, thought Henri, even now, when both were still. Marie's complexion was as fair as Léonore's was dark, and the only likeness between the lovely rosebud face, half hidden by raven-black tresses, and the deer-like grace, even in sleep, of her tawny-haired companion, was the strong air of refinement which no peasant's costume could disguise.

Henri crept back to Guillaume, and the two boys set off, as they always did when it was possible, to bathe before breakfast. Coming back, they found that the girls were awake, and ready for a start. Louis looked brighter, and ate a better breakfast than he had done for the last few days; but at starting Henri offered to carry him at once if he would rather not walk that day.

"Oh no, thank you, Henri," answered Louis, brightly. "I am quite rested now, and can walk a long way."

They kept together nearly all the morning, and in the afternoon began to get into the more cultivated country again. They were anxious to get over rather a longer walk than usual today, as it was Saturday, and they wished to reach a certain village which they had been told of, the first after leaving the hills, before Sunday, as their supply of provisions was running short, and they wanted to make Sunday, as usual, a day of actual rest.

It was very hot, and Louis, who had kept up bravely most of the day, began to flag, and at length asked Guillaume in a whisper if he would carry him a little while. "Henri carried me all the afternoon yesterday," he explained; "and I heard Marie say he would be ill if he did not let you help him. I wish I did not want to be carried," he added, piteously; "but I can't help it, really, Guillaume. My legs get so bad with all this walking that they go right down now and then."

Guillaume went to lift his little brother with a pang of self-reproach. "Guillaume is always ready to carry you, *petit frère*," he said tenderly. "Put your head down on my shoulder, if you will, and go to sleep; or shall I tell you a, story?"

"A story, please, Guillaume," said the little boy, nestling down contentedly; "only, don't you want to go on with Léonore? I shall be able to walk again presently."

Guillaume's eyes filled with tears at this unselfish speech. "You shall not walk again all the afternoon," he said; "and I would rather carry you than do anything else."

"Guillaume! Guillaume!" cried Léonore at that moment, "come on with me, and let us get that old man to the right there to give us some grapes."

"I cannot come," said Guillaume, who had already begun his story; "I am telling Louis the legend of *Les Trois Pommes d'Or.*"

He saw Léonore's face flush angrily as she turned back again to join the others, who had not heard her request. The young countess was not used to be refused by any one whom she delighted to honour. She walked sullenly beside Henri and Marie for a few moments, but they were deep in conversation with each other, and her eyes wandered again to the stalwart, handsome lad in front, with the golden head resting so lovingly upon his shoulder. With a sudden change of mood she turned aside, sprung unaided over a low stone wall, and darted away toward the little vineyard.

Guillaume, who had not noticed her movements, was surprised a few moments after by Léonore's voice saying, almost shyly, "Look, Louis! Such grapes I have got for you." And she held up a large purple cluster of much finer grapes than the usual kinds which they had eaten.

"O Léonore! Thank you," said the child, holding out his hands; "I am so thirsty. Have you got some for yourself and for Marie?"

"Yes, and for Henri too. These are for you and Guillaume," answered Léonore, dropping the bunch into his hands, and running back to the others.

Henri and Marie looked at each other with a smile as they noticed this little scene, and by-and-by Henri offered to take Louis from his brother. Guillaume, however, refused to give up the child, and they went on together through the summer evening, growing rather silent as they all became more or less fatigued.

It grew dark as they entered the little village of Soissons, where they intended to pass the next day; but it was not so much because of the lateness of the hour, as the effect of a coming storm which darkened all the western sky. They had seen it coming for some time, and were congratulating themselves on having reached shelter before it broke. There was but one small inn in the village, and only two tiny bedrooms at the disposal of the children; who were, however, becoming so accustomed to sleep anywhere, that any bed seemed a luxury.

If was scarcely eight o'clock when they had finished their supper, and all the village population were still sitting at the doors, and chatting in little groups. It was very sultry, and every now and then there was a low peal of distant thunder.

Marie went up to put Louis to bed; Guillaume and Léonore sat together on a wooden bench in the little garden of the auberge, and Henri, who was not so tired as the rest, strolled down the village in order to gain information about their route, which he was always obliged to do carefully for fear of exciting suspicion. Marie missed him when she came down, and asked Guillaume where he was.

"Gone down the street; he said he should be back directly," answered Guillaume, with difficulty suppressing a yawn as he rose. "I think I will go to bed now, Marie; I am so sleepy."

He disappeared accordingly, and Marie sat down on the bench to wait for Henri. Léonore did not seem inclined for conversation, and wandered restlessly up and down. A suspicion crossed Marie's mind that Mademoiselle la Comtesse was slightly hurt at Guillaume's departure without any apology, especially as it was the first night since she had joined them that he had not brushed her hair. However, she soon forgot even Léonore's presence when Henri came back, and leant against the trellis-work to answer her inquiries, but with an air of abstraction which struck her immediately.

"Marie," he said at length, rousing himself out of a long reverie, "do you know where we are now?"

"About ten miles from Montauban, you have just told me," answered Marie, wondering.

"Yes; but do you know we are only eleven miles south-west of St. Croix?"

Marie started violently. "St. Croix!" she exclaimed. "I did not know we should pass through anywhere near that part of the country, and surely we must be much nearer the sea-coast than that. Why, only think, Henri, we were but four days driving from St. Croix to St. Louis-de-Linard, and we have now been three weeks walking from thence!"

"Yes; but you must remember that we drove the greater part of the nights too, and went at a great pace. Then coming back, we went at least two days' journey further south than we need have done, as we found afterwards, before we left the Cévennes, and now, you see, we are nearly a whole day's journey beyond St. Croix on our way to Bordeaux."

"I never guessed it; did you, Henri?" asked Marie, her eyes filling with tears.

"No," was the husky answer.

"O Henri!" exclaimed Marie, eagerly, "could we not go to see it tomorrow, just for the last time?"

"No, we must not," said Henri, with an energetic gesture, as if he had been already fighting the question with himself. "See, Marie, it would not be right, for many reasons. Louis must have no more walking than we can help, and it would not be right to leave him here alone all Sunday. Besides, we could hardly walk there and back in a day, and every day is precious to us now. And even if we could go, it would not be safe. We should be certainly recognized, and we do not know who may be there now, or what might be the end of it."

"Yes, I suppose you are right, Henri," admitted Marie, reluctantly. "But oh, Henri," she added, with a sudden burst of tears, "if we could only see Father Gabriel, and not feel so without everything! It is so dreadful to think of that time at home, and I feel as if we had grown so many years older."

"We were children then, Marie, my darling," answered Henri, trying to soothe and comfort his sister, though his own voice grew unsteady. "Don't you remember, *chère petite sœur*, we were weary of our long childhood then, and were ready for our trial? Don't let us be too weak to bear it now it has come."

"You — you were always good," sobbed Marie, leaning against him, and speaking for a moment like the petted, helpless child she had been before their troubles came. "O Henri! What should I do without you?"

They had forgotten all about Léonore for the time, and did not notice in the dusk that she was standing near enough to hear all they said nor that she now ran off with a strange gesture and slipped into the house. Coming up a little later, at Henri's entreaty, Marie found Léonore already in bed, with her long hair streaming over the pillow, and her eyes closed as if in sleep. Marie was too much occupied with her own sad thoughts to wonder at this, and got into bed without even coming near Léonore; but she fell asleep first.

XII

LÉONORE'S EXPEDITION

When Marie awoke, she saw with surprise that Léonore's bed was empty, though it was still very early, and that young lady generally was very difficult to rouse on Sunday, as she considered it only proper, she said, considering that they had walked all the week, to make up the balance of rest on Sunday.

Coming down to the eight o'clock breakfast, she found only the three boys waiting, and inquired of the host if he knew where the other young girl had gone. Mine host, with a shrug of the shoulders, informed them that their sister, as he quietly assumed Léonore to be, had come down more than an hour ago, as soon as the door was open, and had asked for a cup of milk and a roll, saying she was going out for a walk by herself.

"Just like her," said Henri, good-humouredly. "I suppose, then she does not intend to be back till the second *déjeûner*, so we will not wait for her."

Marie looked rather anxious. "I do not like Léonore to be out much alone, Henri. Do you?" she asked, in a lowered tone, as the man withdrew. "She forgets how careful we ought to be, and never thinks of what she says or does whether there are strangers near or not."

"Well, we cannot help it now," answered Henri; "and, I daresay, she has gone out alone into the woods; it would be most like her. In fact, I was going to propose that we should do the same."

"Go out for a walk instead of resting! Think of Louis."

116

"Oh, I did not mean to go for a walk. But, you see, I have been thinking we may get into some trouble if we stay in the inn all day without going to mass. You see," and he spoke in a still lower tone, "she is sure to be all right," said Henri; "the people of this village are all Roman Catholics, and would think it a good deed to inform against heretics if they could. Now, I thought we had better say that we were going to spend the day in the wood, and just go far enough to be out of sight of the villagers, at any rate. We could rest in the wood as well as here."

"Yes; but what about Léonore?" objected Guillaume. "She will come home and find none of us here."

"Yes, that is a difficulty," assented Henri, "but we could write a note, to be given to her if she came back, telling her where to find us."

"It would never do to write a note," put in Marie; "they would know at once that we were not peasant children. A message might do, perhaps."

It was so arranged, and soon after breakfast the four children went out to a little wood behind the village, and spent a very quiet, restful day together. Léonore did not appear, though Guillaume went back twice to the inn to look for her, and when at six o'clock in the evening they all went back, and Marie asked if she had come in, the answer was still "No."

"Where can she be?" exclaimed Marie, beginning to feel alarmed.

"Oh, she is sure to be all right," said Henri; "it is only one of her pranks. Let us have our supper, and then Louis had better go to bed, so as to be fresh for tomorrow."

"There is going to be a storm," said Guillaume abruptly, coming from the window.

"Perhaps it will blow over, as it did last night," suggested Marie, hopefully.

But it did not blow over, for just as they rose from supper a terrific clap of thunder broke quite suddenly over the house, followed by a gust of driving rain. There was a simultaneous

117

exclamation of "Léonore!" as they ran to the window. No Léonore was in sight.

"What *shall* we do, Henri?" asked Marie.

Henri shrugged his shoulders. "One does not know where to go," he said. But Guillaume had already left the room, and they saw him striding down the village in the rain. Henri looked after his brother half ashamed, half amused, and wholly puzzled. "Louis had better go to bed, at any rate," he remarked.

"But perhaps poor Léonore is out in this storm," said Louis, with frightened eyes.

"Well, and if she is, little brother," said Henri, in the tender tone which he always used to Louis, "you cannot go and look for her. Come," he added, raising the little fellow in his arms, "I will carry you upstairs, and you must go to sleep, like a good boy. Marie and I will see after Léonore, and I will promise that you shall find her all right in the morning." Though he spoke so confidently, Henri was by this time getting very anxious, and when he had carried Louis upstairs and left him to Marie, he began seriously to consider the best means of finding Léonore.

It struck him that the host might have noticed which way Léonore took in the morning, and eventually he made out pretty certainly that she had gone almost in an opposite direction to the one in which Guillaume was seeking her. He set off at once, in spite of the furious storm of wind and rain which threatened almost to blow him off his feet, and ran along a path which skirted the wood for some distance, only stopping every now and then to shout for Léonore. By-and-by the path joined on again to a highroad, though not the same as that by which they had come. It still was bordered on one side by the wood, and on the other side by a stretch of rough uncultivated ground, which seemed to reach to the hills which they had passed through the day before.

Henri went on for about a mile along this road without meeting Léonore, and then began to wonder whether he had taken the wrong way after all. It was very strange if she were still farther away at such an hour. Yet where else could she have gone along that road, unless

118

she had lost herself in the uncleared wood? And he had several times gone a little way within it to shout for her. He stopped to consider.

The storm had ceased as suddenly as it began, and was drifting rapidly away, though everything dripped with the heavy rain, and glistened in the brilliant light of the setting sun. Just as Henri had made up his mind to go again and call within the wood, he heard a footstep close in front, and looking up, saw Léonore at length before him. She did not see him, for her eyes were on the ground, and she was walking very wearily. Her hair shone in the sunlight like the dripping leaves, and he could see that her clothing was wet through.

At the sound of Henri's exclamation she looked up, and her face lighted up with pleasure as she said, "Did you come to meet me?"

But Henri's relief was so great that it took the boyish form of anger, and he answered, with a gruffness meant for dignified rebuke: "Well, I think you might have supposed we should be anxious about you, Léonore. What could you mean by going off in that way for the whole day without a word?"

"I am responsible to no one for my actions," answered the young countess haughtily. "I am not under your charge, and it was nothing to you if I chose to absent myself from your company for a day."

"It will be nothing to you, then, I suppose," answered Henri warmly, "if Louis cannot sleep for thinking you are lost, and if Guillaume is laid up with worry and fatigue and cold."

He turned on his heel as he spoke, thoroughly angry, and began to walk home quickly by himself, intending to leave Léonore to her own devices. But he had not gone very far before there was a swift step behind him, and a hand was laid on his arm, while Léonore's voice said entreatingly, "Henri, *mon ami*, do not be angry with me. I was wrong, truly. I might have known; but, indeed, I did not think you would be anxious. I meant to give you pleasure, and now I can only give you pain."

Her brilliant eyes were full of tears, and Henri was divided between sympathy and amazement. He had never seen Léonore so much moved before. But though entirely forgiving what concerned himself, he could not entirely dismiss resentment for his brother. He raised his cap, and said simply, "And I was wrong so to address you, Mademoiselle la Comtesse de Villeneuve."

"Please don't!" pleaded Léonore. "If you knew how I hate myself when I speak so to you, and that I really do not mean it! It is only a bad habit, which no one ever checked in me, and if you knew what I must tell you —" Her voice failed again.

"You have heard bad news somewhere," exclaimed Henri, with a start. "Léonore!" — as a sudden idea flashed across him — "where did you go? To St. Croix?"

Léonore bowed her head in answer, and two great tears rolled down in spite of all her efforts.

"What is it?" asked Henri hoarsely. "Father Gabriel?"

"O Henri, the dragoons have been there!" cried Léonore, in a kind of desperation.

"And he is dead!" answered Henri, with the calmness of a great shock. "Did you hear how it was, Léonore?"

"He was in the church — it was just after service, and they came in suddenly. They bade him come away from the altar, and yield, and he faced them on the steps, and would not. They said he should go free if he would tell them where your father was, and he would not. And then — O Henri! They slew him there before the altar."

"It was the death he would have chosen," answered the boy, almost proudly. "And what then? Did you hear more, Léonore?"

"I talked to an old woman who called herself Mère Benoit," answered Léonore; "and she told me that the wretches were so anxious that your father should not escape them that they did not stay a moment after they had murdered Father Gabriel, and so the rest of the village escaped."

"They were the same, then!" muttered Henri between his clenched teeth.

"She seemed so devoted to you all, and so anxious to know if you had escaped, that I could not help telling her that I had seen you not long ago, and how things had turned out with you. O Henri, did I do wrong?"

"No; she is worthy of trust," answered Henri. "Poor old Benoit! I am glad she has had tidings. Was she not terribly grieved, Léonore?"

"O Henri, it was dreadful! She would scarcely believe me. And most of all she wept for Aurèle. 'He was too good to live,' said she; 'there would never be such another, even at St. Croix.' I do think she would have been content that any one of you should have died, so that Aurèle had been saved."

"And she was right," broke in Henri impetuously. "O Aurèle! Aurèle!" And the boy fairly broke down, and sobbed aloud.

Léonore did not know what to do. To see Henri like this fairly frightened her, and she thought almost with awe of the unknown Aurèle to whom such love was given.

After a few minutes Henri looked up again, and tried to speak as if nothing were the matter. "We are nearly home, Léonore," he said, with a smile that was piteous to see on so young a face. "I hope you are not very tired."

"Oh, it does not matter about me!" cried Léonore under her breath. "O Henri, I am very, very sorry!"

Henri took her hand with an affectionate gesture that did much to console her.

"Thank you," he said simply.

XIII

A NARROW ESCAPE

Meanwhile Marie, too anxious to wait upstairs, was watching for her brothers and Léonore in the salon, which looked out upon the road. There were but two or three people in it while it was still so early, and they smoked their cigars and chatted for some time without seeming to notice her. But Marie could not help fancying that one of them — a dark, ill-favoured looking man — was watching her without appearing to do so, and with no kindly intent. She started when at length the man turned round and addressed her with an affectation of the deepest respect.

"Mademoiselle is anxious for her brother, *n'est-ce pas*? Mademoiselle need not fear; *le jeune gentilhomme* will soon find his way home with the other demoiselle."

Marie looked at the man with as much calm surprise as she could assume, and said in as rustic a tone as possible, "What did you say, Monsieur? My brother has gone after no *jeune gentilhomme* nor demoiselle. It is only Léonore whom he seeks, because we have still some way to walk tomorrow, and she ought to come and go to sleep."

"Why was not Mademoiselle at the mass this morning?" suddenly questioned her tormentor, while the other men listened for the answer.

"Oh, the mass!" said Marie, with a, slight shrug of her shoulders. "One can easily get absolution, and it is not every day poor peasants can spend in the woods." But she flushed up all over her face as she said it. She had never even equivocated before.

Evidently the man was not satisfied, though he said no more to her. But he spoke once or twice to his companions in a low tone, and Marie was sure that she caught the dreaded word "heretic."

She was very much alarmed, and longed more than ever for her brother's return. Evidently these people were bigoted Roman Catholics, and their suspicions were aroused. If they should inform! She felt as if she could not bear to remain any longer in the same room, and as the rain had now ceased, she went out a few steps into the road. Yes; they were in sight — all three. Henri and Guillaume were talking earnestly to each other, and Léonore walked a little behind. Marie ran to meet them; but, in her already alarmed state, she was quick to catch the expression of their faces, and, stopping short, she exclaimed, "O Henri, you have heard bad news!"

"Hush, Marie!" answered her brother anxiously. "Don't you see the street is full of idlers, and this is a Romanist place?"

"Oh, I will not show. Only tell me," said Marie imploringly; "it will be worse when we get indoors."

"Léonore has been to St. Croix," began Henri in a faltering tone.

There was no need to say more. "And it is Father Gabriel?" ended Marie, under her breath.

Henri did not answer; he was struggling for composure. Guillaume came up and took Marie's arm. "Yes; it is Father Gabriel: he died as he lived — a hero."

And there was even a ring of exultation in the boy's tone.

"O Guillaume, was it very bad?" asked Marie, clinging to her brother for support.

"Not very bad. He was shot down on the altar steps."

They told her all that they had heard in a few brief sentences, and then composed their faces as well as possible to enter the auberge, and answer the rough jokes of the men. They went upstairs at once, for all three were dripping wet; but Marie detained Henri for a moment after Guillaume, and drew him into their room, while she told him her fears about the men.

He took the news even more seriously than she expected. "We are among a dangerous set," he said gravely, "and these men would think it a good deed to inform against us."

123

"I am almost sure," said Marie, who was very pale, "that I heard one of them say, 'We will just see if the maire can find out what they are tomorrow.'"

Henri stood in thought for a few moments, and then answered, "Well, Marie, there is no help for it. I am very sorry to give you extra fatigue; but we must leave the place secretly before the people are up. It would never do to run the risk of remaining here."

"O Henri, I am ready; but Léonore — she has walked all day."

"And will walk all night too if it is necessary," said Léonore quickly turning round. "Do you think I would be a drag upon you, even if it were not just as dangerous for me?"

"I am very sorry, Léonore," said Henri, "but if you can walk, I think we must."

"But certainly," answered Léonore, almost angrily, "I shall be ready at whatever time you choose."

"Rest now, then," said the boy, turning to go. "Sleep well, Marie dear, and do not think about getting up; I will wake you when it is time."

But it seemed to Marie scarce half an hour afterwards that she was wakened by a whispered call, and saw Henri in the dim summer night standing dressed by her bedside.

"O Henri! Is it time already?" she inquired sleepily. "Why, it is quite dark."

"It is past two," answered Henri, who had kept watch for the last hour, fearing that if he fell asleep again he might not wake till it was light. "It will soon be light, and these peasants rise so early, we must have a good start. Call Léonore, please, and come into our room when you are ready; I will help Louis."

When the two girls joined him a little later, they found he had arranged everything for their escape. There was a horse-block underneath their window, upon which he could easily let himself down, and then help the others to descend after him.

They conscientiously calculated the amount of their bill, and left the sum upon the rough wooden table in the girls' room. Then Henri noiselessly unfastened the lattice, and with some difficulty managed to squeeze himself through, and dropped lightly on the block.

124

"I don't know how the girls will do it," he whispered anxiously, as Guillaume followed him and nearly pushed him off the block.

Louis, frightened but silent, was next passed through the window, and Guillaume took him from Henri. Then Léonore tried to come through, but found it a more difficult matter than she had thought, and suddenly a bit of the lattice-work broke in her hands with a startling snap, as she plumped down upon the horse-block.

There was an instant's breathless pause, and, as they fancied, a sound within the house. They stood horror-struck, not attempting to run away; indeed, Marie had not yet left the room. However, nothing stirred afterwards, and Henri, growing bolder, whispered, "Now, Marie; there is no time to lose." Léonore moved aside, and Marie, climbing upon the narrow sill, sprung lightly down without a sound. With one consent they set off, running down the village street, and

125

did not stop till they had left it quite behind, and were some way out upon the lonely road.

"I don't think they are after us," panted Léonore, as they paused for a moment to take breath.

"No," said Guillaume. "I looked round as we turned the corner of the road. We were a long way off then, and there was nothing stirring."

Suddenly Henri gave a cry of alarm. "My Testament! I have left it behind."

"No; here it is," gasped Marie, who held it in her hand. "I saw it on your bed just as we were going away, and took it up. You did not leave the pocketbook, did you? I could not see it anywhere."

"No, I have that safe," said Henri, with a sigh of relief, and they walked on more quietly in the gray light before the dawn.

It was a long, weary day, and owing to their secret flight, they had not been able to take any provisions with them. The sun came up with power, and burned fiercely upon the shadeless road, which they dared not leave, as it was so important that they should quickly reach Montauban. About ten o'clock, when they already felt as the day should have passed, they came to a running stream, and lingered some time by its side, trying vainly to satisfy both hunger and thirst with its refreshing water. Soon after this Louis stumbled and fell, and Henri took him up in his arms. So they went on, along that endless, glaring, dusty road.

They tried to sing, but their voices soon died away, and they trudged on silently, with the dogged tread of intense weariness. Marie felt as if they were walking on and on and on in some hideous dream, and when she opened her lips to speak and break the spell, the words refused to come.

Still onward — still the same dusty road — still no sign of habitation. Marie noticed, in a dull, emotionless way, that Léonore's breath came in deep gasps and her lips were blue and parched. No one spoke of resting; there seemed to be no idea left in any of their minds but to walk on until they dropped or reached Montauban. That was the one word that Marie could remember — Montauban —

126

Montauban — Montauban! Her very heart seemed to keep time to the word with dull, slow beats.

At length the road grew wider; houses were seen at some distance on either side and in front — could it be, Marie asked herself, in a curious vague wonder — the town they meant to reach?

Still none of them spoke, though all lifted up their heads, and the flush grew deeper on Léonore's cheek. They had not entered the town when Henri stumbled, and Louis broke the silence by entreating to be set down — he was rested now.

Henri set him down without a word, only keeping hold of his hand. Guillaume did not seem to notice it; he walked with his head bent down and his eyes almost shut; but Marie saw, still in the same dull way, that if it were not for Henri's hand Louis would have fallen every moment.

As they came into the first street of the town they saw at a little distance a baker's shop. Léonore raised her hand and pointed to it, with hungry eyes. With one accord they all pressed on toward it; not hastily, for that was beyond them. Just as they reached its threshold Louis fell down again, and this time he did not rise. He was in a dead faint.

Marie knelt down by his side with a cry which brought the mistress of the shop, a stout motherly Frenchwoman, running to see what was the matter.

"Ah, the poor child!" was her exclamation, as she saw Louis. "Give him to me; you can not lift him, you poor little one. Water — that is the thing. Come in, all of you." And pushing Marie gently aside, she took Louis up in her kind, strong arms, and carried him into a cool back parlour, where she and her equally stout, kind husband, who somehow appeared upon the scene, did their utmost to restore him to consciousness.

It was not long before he opened his eyes, and smiled feebly at Marie, who stood over him.

"Bless his heart! He will be all right in a moment," exclaimed the good-natured women. "What have you been doing to the poor little thing? He is fitter to be in bed than trailing the streets on such a day."

Then looking up her eye fell on Léonore, who had sunk utterly exhausted into a chair, and she continued, "*Comment*, you all look half dead! And strangers! What is it all about? Louis, *mon ami*, fetch some wine, or we shall have five children in a dead faint instead of one."

Louis, the husband, good-humouredly brought some wine, and made them all drink it; though it was doubtful if the sour stuff was the best thing for them. The good-natured woman poured out a string of ejaculations and questions, and as she perceived from their answers that there was something mysterious about the affair, she went off into a series of nods and winks to her husband, which would have amused Marie, if all her senses had not been taken up with the effort to keep from fainting.

She pressed food upon them, and though they could scarcely touch it at first, the healthy craving soon returned, and after making a hearty meal the four elder ones felt more like themselves. Louis lay silent on the sofa, scarcely eating anything, but smiling with a quiet content whenever any one spoke to him.

After their meal Marie drew out the little purse, which Henri kept replenished from his pocket-book, and, with many thanks, would fain have paid for their meal and departed; but the good woman was quite indignant.

"Do you think I am going to take money from a parcel of half-starved children like you?" she exclaimed, with a vehemence which made the boys smile and Léonore flush angrily. "And do you mean to kill the child, that you talk of dragging him one step further today? *Tiens!* Listen to me."

She went and peered into the shop, beckoned out her husband, who had retired thither during their meal, and after his entrance shut the door of communication with an air of great mystery.

"What is it, then, *petite femme?*" asked the great good-natured fellow, with an amused smile.

His wife made a funny little gesture of secrecy, and spoke in an undertone to her guests. "Come," she said, "I know all about it; you need not be afraid of telling me. You are of the Reformed; is it not so?" Henri and Marie looked at one another, and scarcely knew what to answer.

"Come, come," she repeated; "now one sees it, you are noble also. But it is quite safe to confide in Louis and me. See, I will trust you first." And she drew out of an inner pocket a small French Testament, and held it out. "Now Mademoiselle will believe me when I say that we also are of the Reformed."

"You are very good," said Marie, with a grateful impulse. "Henri, let me tell her. It is true, Madame; we are of the Reformed, and we are noble. And the dragoons came upon us by night, and only we children are left of our house, and we fly the country."

"I knew it! I knew it!" cried the good woman, clasping her hands in triumph. "Mademoiselle shall not regret having trusted us; but she must trust us further. See, the house is large, Mademoiselle must have seen worse on her journey, she must permit herself to remain here a day or two until the poor little Monsieur is rested. Shall it not be so, Louis?"

"If these ladies will condescend to remain under my roof, they shall be welcome, and the young gentlemen also," answered the man, with a simple dignity which well became him, and a bow which included both Léonore and Marie.

"We are very much beholden to you," answered Léonore, with a slight hauteur which was perhaps unconscious, and which was lost in Marie's hesitating entreaty that Louis might be put to bed somewhere at once, as they had been walking ever since two o'clock that morning.

"*Comment*, you don't say so!" exclaimed their horrified hostess. "Why, the only wonder is that there is any life at all left in him — Louis, get you back to the shop; you are not wanted now. The young messieurs will doubtless amuse themselves here while Mademoiselle and I take away this poor little one."

"What will you do, Léonore?" asked Marie, seeing a slight frown on that young lady's face.

"Me! Oh, I shall rest here," answered Léonore carelessly, lying back on the rude sofa from which the good woman had just lifted

Louis. "Guillaume cannot you find something to fan me with?" Guillaume obediently came to her side, and sat fanning her more and more lazily, till at length the paper dropped from his hand, and Léonore looking up discovered that both her companions were asleep.

She held up her finger with an amused smile as the baker's wife re-entered with Marie. But the good woman was not so easily repressed, and insisted on every one of them retiring likewise to bed, and staying there till tomorrow morning. In fact, it was already late in the afternoon, and they were only too glad to put off all explanations and arrangements till the next day.

XIV

THE BAKER OF MONTAUBAN

Henri was the first to awake the next morning, and lay lazily regarding the surrounding objects with such a feeling of rest as he had not known for weeks. No one, not even Marie, knew all that he had feared and suffered for the last two or three days. He was, perhaps, the only one of the five who fully realized the difficulties and dangers of their journey, and he had had graver fears for his little brother than he had ventured to put into words, even to Marie. But now, whether it was the effect of bodily and mental exhaustion, or the rest of being once more under a roof which he instinctively felt was safe and friendly, he could feel nothing but content and thankfulness as he lay there in the warm, bright morning, with the early sunlight striking through the unglazed lattice.

Guillaume and he were alone: Marie had entreated that Louis should be in the same room with herself, and Léonore had made no objection, so that there was no small, suffering face on the pillow beside him to recall anxious thoughts. After a time he got out of bed, and guessing by the light and silence of the street that it was still early, he proceeded to dress leisurely, and with as little noise as possible, so as not to wake Guillaume.

It was not long before there began to be a stir outside, and heavy steps, evidently those of the baker and his wife, went down the stairs. Guillaume awoke, rubbed his eyes, and seeing Henri half dressed, sprung out of bed with a sudden fit of energy.

"You need not hurry," said his brother, laughing. "It is quite early, and I do not think we shall start again today."

"Do you know who these people are?" asked Guillaume, stopping short in his dressing.

"No, except that they are of the Reformed religion, and by trade he is a baker.

"How wonderfully good every one has been to us," said Guillaume thoughtfully.

"Yes," answered Henri in a low tone; "God has been with us all the way."

They finished dressing in silence after that, and then Henri went to see if the girls were ready. He met the baker's wife coming out of their room.

"Bonjour, Monsieur," she said pleasantly. "You are early a stir; but the coffee is ready downstairs."

"Is my sister — are the young ladies dressed?" asked Henri.

"Monsieur will find his sisters ready to descend; but for the young Monsieur his brother, I have begged Mademoiselle to let him have coffee upstairs, and remain in bed for a while."

Henri pressed on into his sisters' room: he had quite grown to look upon Léonore in that light, and he was anxious about Louis. However, the little fellow looked very well and happy in his fresh clean bed; but owned that he was very tired, and would like to be left upstairs.

So the four others went downstairs, and won the good people's hearts completely by their pleasant, respectful manners and gratitude for the kindness shown them. The rolls were all made and sent out already; but there were still some cakes to see after, and the young ladies begged to be allowed to help. The two boys at first stayed to watch; but after a little while Henri slipped away to see after Louis.

He opened the door very carefully, in case the child was asleep, and at first he thought it was so. Louis was lying back with his eyes shut; he was very much flushed, and his breathing came quick and short.

"Louis!" said Henri softly.

Louis turned round with a quick, restless movement, and opened his large blue eyes; but they had a strange vacant look. "Henri," he said vaguely, not looking at his brother, "is it time to go on again already?"

"No, Louis," answered Henri very tenderly, though he felt very much alarmed; "we are going to rest today."

"Rest — rest," murmured the little fellow, turning back again. "When is Mamma coming?"

"Do you want Marie, dear? I will go and call her."

"Mamma too! — Mamma!" insisted Louis.

Henri slipped quietly downstairs, and went to look for Madame Argent, as he had discovered that their hostess was called. He found her in the parlour, where she did most of her light cooking, cutting some potatoes into strips, to fry for the *déjeûner à la fourchette*. She smiled and nodded to Henri, and asked what she could do for him.

"I am grieved to disturb you, Madame," began Henri; "but if you could come up for a moment to look at my brother: I am afraid he is going to be ill."

She looked at him sharply for a moment, and then said gently, "He is that already, Monsieur. But come; let us see what we can do."

She went upstairs at once, followed by Henri. Louis lay just in the same position, and did not look up at their approach. Madame Argent felt his pulse and the palm of his hand; upon which he roused himself to ask faintly for water, and seemed revived when Henri gave him some.

"I am so tired, Henri," he sighed, as he fell back again. "Is Marie asleep?"

"No, dear. Do you want her?"

"Ask her to come and sing to me, please."

They went down again, and Henri paused to ask anxiously what Madame thought of his brother.

"Oh! He will do well enough, I hope," she answered cheerfully. "He is just altogether worn out, that is all, and no wonder. Please God, a few days' rest will set him all right again."

A few days! The words were enough in themselves to make Henri very thoughtful as he went in search of his sister.

She came at once, and was shocked and alarmed to see the change which an hour or two had apparently wrought in their little brother. She and Henri, with occasional visits from the other two, spent the day with him, much of it in absolute silence, as Louis fell into restless sleep. There was no talk of going on that day, nor the next, which was passed much in the same way.

On the third day he seemed much better; was quiet, and able to think and talk clearly. He even spoke of going on, and declared that he should be quite well enough to do so tomorrow.

"What do you think, Madame?" said Henri, following her into the garden alone that evening. "Will it be too soon? Time is so very precious to us.

"So is the life of Monsieur your brother, I should hope," exclaimed the good woman, almost angrily.

Henri gasped as if he had been struck. "His life! You told me you did not think there was any danger, Madame," he exclaimed.

"Nor is there, so long as he lies quiet in bed; but if you take him up now, and set him to walk ten — five — even one mile a day, *ecoutez*! his life is not worth that!" — with an expressive snap of her fingers. "The poor little fellow!" she added with a half sob, which Henri did not hear in his consternation.

"What are we to do?" he said at length.

"I will tell you what you must do," she exclaimed suddenly, turning round upon him. "But stay; I can explain nothing without my Louis. If Monsieur will wait one moment."

She vanished as she spoke into the house, and came back in a moment with the burly, good-natured man, who looked, as on the former occasion, much embarrassed by his wife's vigorous measures. "Tell him — tell the young Monsieur, *mon ami*," she cried with the same sob in her voice, "tell him what you and I settled last night."

Monsieur Argent fidgeted, and seemed uncertain how to begin, while Henri waited in dreary astonishment. "Monsieur sees," he said at length, "that it has pleased God to afflict us — that we have no child."

"But we had one — the angel!" broke in his wife. "A little Louis; just the age of the little Monsieur, when he died of the sweating sickness."

134

Monsieur Argent bowed in grave assent to his wife's speech, and continued: "Therefore, as it seems a matter of great importance to Monsieur that he should reach Amsterdam without delay, and as one sees clearly that the little Monsieur will not be able to continue his journey for some weeks —"

"Months!" put in his wife.

And with the same grave bow of assent, he proceeded: "My wife and I are hoping that Monsieur will see fit to intrust his little brother to our care until such time as it shall please God that they may rejoin each other in safety."

Having delivered himself of this speech, Monsieur Argent heaved a deep sigh, and looked at his wife for approbation.

Henri was thunderstruck. "Leave Louis — with you!" he stammered. "It is impossible; he would break his heart."

"He has too much spirit for that," cried the good wife indignantly. "Ah, Monsieur, believe me, none can so fitly care for a child as a mother, even if the child be noble and the mother of the people."

"Indeed, I meant nothing of that sort," exclaimed the lad hastily. "I only meant — pardon me, Madame, I do indeed see how kind you are; but it cannot be — we cannot spare our Louis!"

Madame Argent would have begun fresh explanations and entreaties, but her husband, with a tact rare in a man of his stamp, signed to her to be silent, and drew her away. "You will think of it, Monsieur," he said in departing. "For the sake of Monsieur's brother, I would pray him to do so."

They went indoors again, and Henri wandered down the little garden in the sweet warm twilight of early autumn, through the orchard, where the fruit trees bent beneath their glowing burden, down to the little rivulet which flowed murmuringly at the end of the orchard.

He stood there on the brink, unconscious of everything around him, not even capable of connected thought, while the words seemed to echo in his mind, "If you take him away, he will die." But how to leave him behind! His little Louis, the pet and darling of the family, whose future life he and Marie had so often fancifully

135

imagined together, and without whom they should all feel lost. How to leave him with these people! Very good people, doubtless, but still only a baker and his wife, whom they had only known three days. He was just repeating to himself that it was impossible, when he heard his name softly called, and the next moment Marie stood beside him, with her dark eyes shining in the dim light as she looked up in his face.

"Henri, is anything the matter?" she said in a startled tone. "When I came downstairs just now to find you, Monsieur and Madame Argent were talking in the parlour. Madame was crying, and when I asked her for you, she said, 'He is in the garden, Mademoiselle. Go and persuade him to do as we have said; it is the only way to save the little Monsieur's life.' What does it mean, Henri? What does she want you to do?"

"She wants us to leave Louis behind, to be brought up with them," answered Henri, hoarsely and abruptly.

Marie started with a frightened gasp. "O Henri! Must we really?"

"*Must!*" echoed the boy. "*Can* we give him up, we who have promised to stand by each other to the last? I cannot do it, Marie."

"But, Henri," suggested Marie timidly, "if we ought. What do you think Mamma would wish us to do?"

"Do you think she would like him to be brought up as a baker's son?" asked Henri bitterly. "He, a De St. Croix of St. Croix, to be known as Louis Argent, and run the streets with the *canaille* of Montauban!"

"These good people would never let him do that," answered Marie, with a little hush of indignation. "See you, they never forget that we are noble, and they will take care that Louis does not learn bad ways. And as for the rest, I think our father would say that a true noble would never forget his birth, and that it was not what he was obliged to do, but what he was himself, that mattered. Why, Henri, have not we ourselves been wandering like beggars for the last three weeks? And do we feel ourselves a whit less noble?"

"We know it only a means to an end," muttered Henri. "We are on our way to the land where we shall be able to resume our right place; but to leave Louis here —"

"They did not mean to keep him away forever; they would let us send for him when we could?" questioned Marie eagerly.

"So they say; but who can tell when that will be?" answered Henri bitterly.

"If it may never be, then it will be because something has happened to us," suggested Marie softly. "Would he not be more out of harm's way to appear as the child of a baker, whom few, it seems, know as belonging to the Reformed religion, and all respect?"

"So you would be content," cried the lad, turning almost savagely upon her; "you would let him go, our little Louis, and go on just as happily if he were not with us?"

"Henri!" The anguish of that faint cry struck Henri to the heart as her hand slipped from his arm, and Marie sunk down in a burst of bitter weeping. He knelt down by her, covering her with caresses, and pouring out self-reproaches for his unkindness. Marie's tears, once yielded to, were difficult to check; but she tried hard, and looked up at length with a bright April smile.

"Let us leave it to Louis himself," she said; "he is no baby now, and it is only fair he should have some say in it."

"Very well," said Henri at once; "we will leave it to him — but not tonight, Marie. Do you think so?"

"Oh no; we will not disturb him tonight," said Marie. "He might not sleep after it, and it is getting late."

As she spoke they heard Léonore calling them, and saw her white dress coming through the darkness. Guillaume was with her, and they seemed full of fun and laughter.

"Louis is fast asleep," said Léonore as she came up, "so Guillaume and I came out to look for you. What are you discussing so soberly this beautiful night?"

The light question met with an answer for which the speaker was little prepared. Henri gravely told them what had been proposed for the little one.

Léonore was furious at the notion. She scouted the idea of Louis' life being in danger, and declared it was all a plot of these people, a scheme to get him for their own, and was Louis to be sacrificed to such meanness? She went on till Henri himself was fain to take up the defence of the good people who had so kindly sheltered them. Guillaume listened in perfect silence, without even an exclamation of surprise. Marie slipped her hand into his, and he kept it there, but gave no other sign of feeling.

They scarcely noticed how late it was growing, till Monsieur Argent himself came down the orchard path, and with much hesitation submitted to Monsieur that it was getting late — when people had to rise early for the rolls — Henri rose at once, and they all went in to bed.

XV

Louis' Choice

"Marie, may I come in?"

It was nearly noon on the following day, and Henri stood at the door of Marie's room, where Louis still lay. As he entered he could not help seeing that the little fellow looked more pale and fragile than ever. His golden hair fell back from a face whiter than the clean but unbleached cotton upon which it lay, and his eyes shone with the light of fever; yet he turned round with a bright smile of welcome for his brother, and held out a hand so thin and wasted that Henri could have cried over it. Only Marie was in the room with him. Guillaume had gone out for a long walk by himself, and Léonore was gathering apples with Madame Argent in the orchard.

"Do you feel better today, Louis darling?" asked Henri, as he sat down beside him.

"Oh yes, thank you!" said Louis, with the same bright smile.

"He always says he is better," said Marie, wistfully; "but just now he tried to walk across the room, and —" She stopped, fearful of giving way to a burst of tears.

"And I couldn't," said Louis, taking up the sentence with that strange, quiet cheerfulness. "Isn't it odd, Henri? Because I feel really much better than I did the last two or three days. I suppose I shall get rested by-and-by, if I lie still long enough; only I am so sorry, because I'm afraid it is only for me you are waiting now."

"It is not that we mind the waiting" said Henri, hoarsely; "only, do you know, Louis, Madame Argent thinks it may be a long time before you are strong enough to walk again."

"Does she think I am going to die?" asked the child, with an actual light of eagerness in his beautiful blue eyes.

"Oh no, no!" burst from his brother and sister at once. It was all they could say, and Marie knelt down by the window, that Louis should not see the struggle in her face.

"I'm rather sorry, I think," Louis went on. "I thought about it all last night, when I was so vexed because I was keeping you all, and I saw Madame Argent go out of the room crying, and I thought if I did die it would be all right, because I should only go to Mamma and Papa and Aurèle, and then you would not have to carry me all the way."

"O Louis! Please don't talk so!" burst out Marie. "You are not going to die; Madame Argent says so."

"Then how long shall we all have to wait here?" asked Louis in a resigned tone.

"Well, that depends —" said Henri, hesitatingly.

It was very touching to see the big, handsome bronzed lad bending over the slight, fragile, golden-haired child with such tender sorrow and care.

"What should you think, Louis, of staying here to get well with Madame Argent, while we went on to Amsterdam, and then sent for you in some easier way?"

Louis gave a violent start; his cheeks flushed painfully, and the great blue eyes were turned entreatingly toward his brother.

"Go on without me!" he said.

"Oh no, Louis darling, we won't!" sobbed Marie, falling on her knees beside him. "We will never leave you, if you don't like it."

Henri put his hand on Marie's shoulder with a whispered "Hush!" though his own voice was husky as he spoke to Louis.

"You must think about it, Darling, and be quite sure we will not leave you, even for a time, unless you wish it. Madame Argent said it would be the best way, and we proposed to ask you; but nothing shall separate us, my Louis, if you cannot bear it."

The child buried his face in the pillow without a word, and no one spoke for a minute or more, for Henri signed silence to his sister.

Then there was a knock at the door, and Léonore's voice said, rather timidly, "Henri and Marie, are you not coming down to the *déjeûner*?"

"Yes; go down," said a small, smothered voice from the pillow. "Go away, even Marie, please, and when you come up again I will tell you."

They went down and left him alone; but as soon as the meal was over the brother and sister hurried upstairs again, and came quietly into the room.

Louis turned round with his quiet, bright smile. "I have thought about it, Marie," he said, as they came up to the bed. "I shall stay."

Marie knelt down and kissed him, unable to speak.

"I think Papa would have said so," he went on in the same dreamy way. "I would rather have died, I think, unless dying hurts very much; for then I should only have gone from you and Guillaume to Papa and Mamma and Aurèle. And now I shall be all alone. But I don't mind it much, Marie — never mind." For he guessed that Marie was crying, though he could not see her face.

"Children de St. Croix!" he murmured, half to himself. "I don't remember much of the old days; but do you remember one Sunday Papa was talking about that, and we asked how we could be Soldiers of the Cross, and he said we could not choose; God would show us each our own way?"

The two elders listened with astonishment, almost with dismay. To hear their little Louis, who had always seemed even more childish than his years, talking in this way — what did it mean? Neither of them spoke, and Louis turned away again with a deep sigh.

"I am so tired!" he said. "I think I could go to sleep again now, only you won't go away, will you? I should like to see you as long as I can, and you ought to start tomorrow."

"Oh, not tomorrow — not so soon as that!" cried Marie.

"Yes, tomorrow," insisted the child quietly. "Is it not right, Henri?"

"I suppose so," said the elder brother, very sadly.

They moved away then to the window, where Louis could still see them, and after a little while they thought he had fallen asleep, but he still seemed restless, and at last asked where Guillaume was.

"I will call him," said Marie.

When she opened the door, she was surprised to find Léonore crouched on the narrow landing outside in an attitude of suspense. She sprung up as Marie came out, asking, in an excited whisper, "O Marie! What have you settled?"

"He is going to stay," said Marie simply, "and he wants Guillaume."

"I'll find him!" and Léonore vanished down the narrow stairs in a moment. Marie went back and told Louis that Léonore had gone to find Guillaume, and then she and Henri sat down in the window-seat again and waited. It was nearly an hour before Léonore came back and admitted Guillaume, white and trembling, but resolutely calm, and then lingered beseechingly at the half-closed door, until Marie beckoned to her to come in also.

So they all sat together that long bright afternoon, the four talking in whispers at first, while Louis slept. They would have avoided speaking of their departure, when he awoke; but they soon found that it was the only thing he seemed to care to talk about, and every detail, so far as they knew, of their morrow's journey was settled by Louis' bedside. Madam Argent left them to themselves. She guessed pretty well how matters were going on.

But the longest day comes to an end at last, and so did that long bright autumn day, which none of the children ever forgot. It grew too late to keep Louis talking any longer. They went down for a short time to make arrangements with Monsieur and Madame Argent. The short night passed, and the morning had come.

They were to start very early, and instead of the usual coffee and rolls, Madame Argent had prepared a meat breakfast for them at seven o'clock. One or other of them had been hanging about Louis since six. He had been carried down to see them at breakfast and now was propped up again at his bedroom window, whence he could see them go down the orchard path and across the field, before the road must take them out of sight. Here they all came round him, to say goodbye for the last time. Marie was biting her lip to keep back the tears which she had prayed for help to repress. Louis must see her for the last time with a bright face.

Louis was smiling too, though there was a quiver about his lip. "We have not had any singing this morning," he said wistfully, as they all came in. "Couldn't we have one song before you go?"

Could they? The elder ones exchanged glances at this simple and yet, it seemed, impossible request. But they could not deny Louis, and Léonore, seeing that they could not trust themselves to speak, bent forward and asked Louis what they should sing.

"Sing the song of the Soldiers de St. Croix," he said.

It was the oldest of all their songs that he asked for — one that they used never to be weary of singing, even when the words had little meaning for them, in the old home at St. Croix. Tradition said that it had been composed on the march by an old Aurèle de St. Croix who went to Palestine in the first Crusade. They had sung it almost every day since they left St. Louis-de-Linard, and no one wondered at Louis' choice. Léonore began it, her rich young voice sounding alone at first, but one after another they all joined in, and the old spirit kindled in them as they sang:

It is true the road is rough and dreary;
It is true our feet are sore and weary;
Parched with thirst, our lips are cracked and bleeding
Scarcely can we see the banner leading:

Yet lift your hearts up, comrades, comrades,
Lift your hearts up to the Lord;
Lo! For each one of us His soldiers
There's a crown of glory stored.
Much shall it profit us, comrades, comrades,
If we count this world as loss;
For there's a paradise beyond it
For His Soldiers of the Cross.

Let us watch — the post is worth maintaining;
Let us fight — the strife is worth the gaining;
Till the sword is struck from arms unslackened,
And we drop down dead in deserts blackened.

Yet lift your hearts up, comrades, comrades, etc.

Unto death we bear the cross of Jesus,
Unto death we strike and know He sees us,
After death is time for peace end pleasure,
After death comes rest beyond our measure.

Then lift your hearts up comrades, comrades,
Lift your hearts up to the Lord;
Lo! For each one of us His soldiers
There's a crown of glory stored.
Much shall it profit us, comrades, comrades,
If, for life-long toil and loss,
We hear Him say, "Well done, my Soldiers,
My brave Soldiers of the Cross!"

Even Louis found strength to join in that chorus, and when it was over he lay back content. "Say goodbye now," he said.

Léonore came and kissed him, and then drew back again, but could not bear to leave the room. And the sister and brothers kissed each other with long lingering kisses and resolute smiles, and then took up their cross and turned away.

Down through the orchard they went, each one lingering and looking up to the little casement where the golden head shone so brightly, and the blue eyes followed them so wistfully, and the little hand fluttered a signal of goodbye. At the corner of the field they stopped to take a farewell look, and then with one accord they turned and ran till they could run no longer.

Late that night, after singing but one hymn, and that brokenly, they lay down once more by a campfire to rest. Marie, after thankfully watching Henri fall asleep — he had not slept the whole of the preceding night — stayed for a long time talking in a low tone to Guillaume, who, in one of his rare fits of unreserve, was pouring out all his self-reproach for his late neglect of Louis and unfair treatment of Henri.

"There never was such a fellow for thinking of every one except himself," he concluded. "O Marie! I wish I were like him."

"Hush, then, my Guillaume," said Marie softly. "Henri would not like you to say that. Don't you remember Aurèle used to say we must not try to be like one another, but like Christ?"

"Please God, so I will," said the boy solemnly.

In the silence which followed, Marie heard something which sounded like a moan from Léonore, whom she had fancied to be asleep. Guillaume heard it too, and half-started up. Marie went to her, and was almost frightened, for Léonore was crying bitterly, her whole frame heaving with long deep-drawn sobs. Marie had never seen her cry before.

"Léonore! O Léonore! What is it?" she asked, with her arm round the sobbing girl.

Léonore clung tightly to her, and gasped out, "O Marie! Don't hate me. Love me a little, for I am so miserable. I have no one in all the world, and it makes me nearly mad to see you all together; but I did not mean to take Guillaume away from Louis."

"Nor did you, Darling," said Marie, with her tenderest caresses. "Louis loved you — we all love you, Léonore."

Guillaume had heard his own name, and came forward. "Léonore," he said, with a trembling voice, "you make me more miserable by thinking so. Pray, don't cry. Be our sister. Let us comfort each other."

Léonore caught him by the hands and kissed him for the first time, with Marie's arm still round her. Then Guillaume crept back again, and Marie and Léonore fell asleep together.

XVI
CAUGHT AT LAST

Two or three days passed, and the natural cheerfulness of the French temperament reasserted itself. But still they missed Louis daily, hourly; missed him in every way, though no one would have owned that they got on with their journey more quickly now that they had left Louis behind.

Léonore was a great help to them all. Her mischief was almost entirely laid aside, and she seemed to have suddenly become far more womanly; but her high spirits kept them cheerful in spite of themselves, and they often said to each other how fortunate it was that they had met with her.

It was midday, and they were coming into a little town, such as they frequently passed through now. They intended merely to make a few purchases, and then to go some way on the other side of the town before dining, as they had not walked very far that morning. Generally, they went as quickly and quietly as possible through anything like a town. But from habit they were getting a little careless about keeping out of the way, and seeing a crowd round a fussy little man, who was haranguing loudly on the steps of a large building, curiosity made them linger to hear what was the matter.

He had a table in front of him, and one person after another came up, it seemed, for the purpose of signing something that lay upon it. Before they did so, however, he recited to them in a loud voice the subject of the paper, and as the reciting took up at least three minutes, and the signing — or rather marking, for there was scarce one in all that assembly who could write — scarcely one, the effect was as of a continued discourse.

The four children got entangled in the crowd before they were aware, as they came nearer in the hope of catching what was said. Léonore was first, closely followed by Henri; Guillaume and Marie got separated from them a little way; indeed, Marie did not quite see what they were doing. She was busy in a mental calculation of the money in her purse after their recent purchases, and did not notice particularly what was going on around her.

It flashed upon Henri, as he came near enough to hear, that this was some oath the people were taking, probably one of which he heard several people speak of late — an oath of obedience to the King and Pope, and a declaration of faith in the Roman Catholic religion according to them. In a moment he saw how heedless they had been, and with a hasty whisper to Léonore, he tried to draw her away.

But he was too late. The man had seen him, and, leaning forward, called to him to come up and sign the paper. Henri still tried to withdraw; but this only excited suspicion. Two or three hands were stretched out to prevent him, and the man repeated his demand. He paused for an instant to reflect upon his answer, and in that moment Léonore pressed forward to the table.

"What would you with my idiot page, Sir?" she asked, with a resumption of her old haughty manner. The man was evidently surprised, and then, with a true French shrug of the shoulders, handed the pen to Léonore.

"No, Mademoiselle," he answered, "this is no oath for idiots, but for all who love God and the King, whether noble or simple. Mademoiselle is doubtless able to read the paper and to sign her own name. My orders are that all in this town shall sign it before the night has passed."

"Read it to me," said Léonore, feigning not to understand.

Such ignorance was often found then even among the upper classes. The little man, nothing loath, took up the paper again and read it through. It was just such an oath as Henri had feared, one that no true Protestant could subscribe to with a clear conscience.

Léonore listened with the utmost gravity to the end, and then bowed low.

"One's ignorance becomes a pleasure when one hears Monsieur read," she remarked with great politeness. "Yes, I quite understand. I am much obliged to Monsieur."

She bowed again, and made a movement to withdraw, with such calm assurance that the little man stared, and had almost suffered her to go. With a sudden resolve, however, he signed to those around to prevent her, while he said, "Pardon me; but Mademoiselle has not taken the oath."

"*Comment!*" exclaimed Léonore, with well-acted surprise, "I have heard Monsieur read it."

"Yes, yes; but that is not all. Mademoiselle must have the goodness to lay her hand on this book here, and repeat these words after me." And he ran off a short formula of unconditional acceptance.

Léonore remained silent.

"*Comment!* Mademoiselle does not mean that she refuses to take the oath!"

There was an instant's pause, and then Léonore answered boldly, "Yes; I do refuse it."

The crowd moved with eager expectation. All eyes were turned toward Léonore. She meanwhile was quivering with anxiety to know whether Henri had obeyed her imperious gesture, and withdrawn with his brother and sister; but she would not look round, for fear of drawing attention to them.

"Take her away," commanded the little man at length. He was new to this sort of work, and having been appointed to a very loyal district, had never met with resistance before. "Take her, and her idiot page also; let them be carefully guarded in the bureau until tomorrow, when they will return with me to Marmande, to go before the officers there."

Thus Léonore knew that Henri was still behind her, and they were marched off without being able to exchange a word. But both noticed that Guillaume and Marie had disappeared.

On seeing that Léonore was "in for it," Henri had turned to look for Guillaume and Marie, and had been able to sign unperceived to the former. Guillaume took in the state of affairs at a glance, and acted promptly.

"Where's Henri?" Marie had asked, as she looked up at length.

"On there," said Guillaume, leading her in quite a different direction. "Let us make haste; we must catch them up to them."

He hurried her on down the street for some way, and then turned aside into a narrow byway, before she exclaimed, "Guillaume, you must be wrong. There is no sign of Henri or Léonore. Let us go back and look for them."

"I will go," said Guillaume hurriedly; "they must be close behind, at any rate. Wait here for me, please Marie, or we shall all be losing each other." He ran off without giving her time to remonstrate, and made his way as quickly and cautiously as possible to the spot he had just left. His worst fears were confirmed. Henri and Léonore were being led away prisoners.

He mingled with the crowd which pressed round them, taking care not to excite suspicion by his looks. For one instant he managed to get close to Henri, and felt something pressed into his hands, though Henri's head was turned away. It was the packet of papers and money. Guillaume thrust it into his bosom and followed the crowd for a few steps further, till they came to a small official building, whether a prison or merely a justice court he could not make out, as only the prisoners and a couple of gendarmes, who had acted as their guard, were allowed to enter. Guillaume waited till the door had actually shut upon them, and then, slipping aside, ran as soon and as fast as he dared to Marie.

She was waiting for him in considerable anxiety. "O Guillaume!" she exclaimed, "I thought you would never come, and I should have gone after you, only I feared we should miss one another. But why are you alone? Where have you left Henri and Léonore?"

"They are taken," said Guillaume abruptly, as he leaned against the wall and covered his face with his hands.

She scarcely understood. "Taken!" she repeated, and then, as the truth dawned upon her, she cried, "Guillaume, Guillaume, you do not mean that they have been arrested?"

He did not answer.

She leaned back, also overcome. The blow was so sudden, and, after such a long time of safety, so unexpected.

"How was it?" she asked at length. "I saw nothing. Was it that man who was calling out on the steps?"

Guillaume nodded.

"And where are they taken? O Guillaume, did you find out?"

"I do not know what the place is, but I saw them go in. We must wait now; we can do nothing till the streets are quieter, and then I will show you the place."

They went outside the town into some fields, and tried to eat some food, but it was almost impossible. They wandered restlessly up and down, and at length went back into the town again.

XVII

In the Prison

Meanwhile Henri sat alone in the prison, for he had been confined in a separate room from Léonore, and had not been able to speak to her since their arrest. He intended to play the part which Léonore had assigned to him, of her idiot page, as long as possible, though he was not quite sure how she intended it to benefit either of them.

It will easily be imagined that he felt very miserable. The trials of the last few weeks had done much to depress his naturally buoyant spirits, and thus he was more cast down by his present position than he would otherwise have been. He knew well enough now what an arrest meant for those who would not recant. At the mildest it meant a convent for the girl, the galleys for the boys; beyond that he did not care to think. He sat with his head on his hands, trying to realize what it would be, trying to school himself to face the only too probable fact that he should never see his brothers and sister again. The scalding tears forced themselves slowly between his fingers as he sat there, and he dashed them passionately away. Then he threw himself upon his knees, and spent his time in alternate prayers for help, and thanksgiving that Marie was not there, and that Guillaume had the packet safe. As for the Testament, Marie had been carrying it at the time, so that too was safe.

The day passed wearily away. Only once a gendarme came to him, and brought some food; but mindful of his part, Henri did not speak a word to him. Toward evening, when it was getting dusk, he heard some one whistling beneath his window outside: it did not look into the street, but into a narrow passage at the back. He listened eagerly; it was the tune of the Soldiers of the Cross, and he knew it must be Guillaume. The window was too high for him to see so near underneath it; but he waited for a pause, and took up the tune himself. They answered each other in this way for some minutes, and then Guillaume ceased — he supposed for fear of exciting suspicion.

As night came on, and still no one appeared, he came to the conclusion that he was to spend it just where he was, and wondered anxiously what Léonore was doing. At length he fell into an uneasy slumber, and so the night passed, and another clear, beautiful morning dawned.

It was still very early when he was taken out of his prison by two gendarmes, and he found a small body of them waiting outside, who had evidently been sent from the next town for the purpose of escorting the prisoners. Léonore was already in front, riding on a small horse, with a mounted gendarme on either side of her. She did not look round at him, and he tried to appear as vacant and silly as possible.

It was a great relief to him to find that the town to which they were bound was a stage further on their way to Bordeaux. He could scarcely have explained why, as he had not the slightest hope of release; but he liked to think that they were still going on. Besides, he knew that Guillaume and Marie would be sure to have found out where they were going, and would follow them as long as possible.

It was late in the afternoon when they reached Marmande, and they were kept waiting for some minutes in the broiling sun while one of the men waited on the council for orders. Finally, they were taken to the common prison, but still were confined separately and alone, and informed that they would go before the magistrate on the morrow.

Henri received the news with indifference. He was so far exhausted by this time as to imagine that he had made up his mind to the worst, and could receive it with stoical calmness: only he did want very much to know where Léonore was, and how she was feeling, and Guillaume and Marie, were they safe, and did they know where he was? Ah! It was of no use to affect indifference; the bowed head and locked hands told a different tale — when he was alone.

The day came, and the time for the trial. Henri was summoned roughly about noon, and conveyed a short way down the street to the council-room, where the judge for that province was then sitting. It was a large, poorly furnished room; the judge, a gentle-looking old man with white hair, sat at a table at the farther end, with a clerk writing at a smaller table just beside him. As he entered the room his eyes fell upon Léonore. She had just been brought in, and was already undergoing her examination. Henri, as he listened, was astonished by the readiness and ingenuity of her answers. She gave her real name and rank, and told them what was the truth, that she was flying from her relatives, who were Roman Catholics. She allowed it to appear that she was travelling alone with her page, as she called Henri, and threatened them in no very gentle terms with the vengeance of her powerful relatives if she were not treated in a befitting manner, or bestowed anywhere but with them. The judge knew well enough that if her tale were true it was the only course open to him to pursue, and that his wisest plan was to treat her with all respect until her relatives could be communicated with. He therefore ordered that she should be removed to a convent, and that the nuns should have charge of her until orders arrived from Monsieur de Villeneuve.

He then beckoned Henri to approach and proceeded to interrogate him. The lad, mindful of his part, answered not a word for some time, but stared blankly at the judge. Suddenly, as sometimes will happen even on the most serious occasion, a keen sense of the ludicrous side of his position struck him, and it was with the greatest difficulty that he restrained himself from a burst of laughter.

The truth was, he was thoroughly unhinged. He felt as if he were in a dream: the judge's voice sounded far off, and yet he noticed everything, even to the motes in the sunbeam which came in from the window high above, and shone on Léonore's tawny hair as she

153

stood a little aside with her attendants, endeavouring, with tolerable success, to conceal how anxious she was about Henri's examination.

He knew how important it was — how the least suspicion of his sanity might be fatal to him now, and yet he felt as if he were losing all control over himself. At length the idea struck him that, being such an insane thing to do, it might not matter whether he gave way or not, so long as he laughed foolishly. He had not the least idea what the judge was saying by this time — the room felt as if it were turning round — when suddenly he startled them all, even Léonore for a moment, by a loud and prolonged burst of laughter.

The judge spoke to him angrily; he knew that, but only laughed the more. He became conscious that the judge was looking thoroughly puzzled; that Léonore spoke sharply of the folly of wasting time on an idiot who had but one idea — to do as she bade him, and then — and then he saw an evil-looking man stoop down to the judge and say in a low, distinct tone, evidently meant for him to hear, "Try what the torture-room will do, Monsieur!"

His senses were all alive in a moment, and he had almost stopped laughing. If he had, it would have been fatal. But the pause was only momentary; the next instant he saw the trap, and laughed the louder.

The man looked baffled, and yet not wholly satisfied. He was about to make some other suggestion, when Léonore broke in again, "*Comment*, Monsieur! Is the Comtesse de Villeneuve to be kept waiting here all day? When you have quite satisfied yourself that there is no more sense than heresy in my poor lad there, perhaps you will allow us to withdraw to this convent of yours, where I trust I may be able to support life until my kinsman appears."

"It is impossible that Mademoiselle can retain the services of her page in the convent," answered the judge testily. "He must be confined separately."

"And why so?" demanded Léonore with well affected indignation and surprise. "Have you found him guilty of heresy? If I may not keep my own attendant in the convent because, forsooth, your nuns cannot suffer even the semblance of a lad, he shall go and bring me my own woman from Villeneuve."

"If the lad is an idiot, he can scarce be trusted with a message," observed the dark man who stood at the judge's elbow. His eyes were fixed on Henri, who, though his heart beat loudly with suspense, affected to be indifferently counting his buttons.

"Does not even a dog know its master?" retorted Léonore in a tone of contempt. "If I give him a token, and say but the name, you shall see he will bring me my woman quicker than any of your gendarmes could do it were the dragoons at their heels!"

This speech provoked a grim smile from most of the audience, and then there was a pause, while the judge, the dark man, and the clerk conferred together in low, brief sentences.

At length, apparently against the opinion of one of them, but seconded by the man who acted as clerk, the judge turned round and signified that the request might be granted; but that the message must be given, and the lad despatched at once, in his presence.

"The sooner the better," answered Léonore indifferently. "I will send her something from my person; she will understand the more quickly." She unfastened a silken handkerchief from her neck as she spoke, and held it out toward the judge. "Perhaps Monsieur will like to see for himself that there is no dark heretical scheme concealed in it," she added, with a curl of scorn on her handsome lip.

The dark man took the handkerchief from her hand, and gravely examined every part of it. Having apparently satisfied himself, he suddenly held it out to Henri, with the words, "There, go, and be thankful that you have got off so easily."

Henri was ready-witted enough to stare vacantly at the handkerchief, without offering to take it. Léonore burst into a mocking laugh, "It is a good animal, you see. Give me the handkerchief, and rest content."

The man, still narrowly watching them both, handed the handkerchief back to Léonore, who approached Henri, and placed it in his hand. "*Ecoutez!*" she said slowly and deliberately, looking straight into his eyes. "Take it to Madame Bernard, Villeneuve." She repeated the name twice, and Henri nodded several times with every sign of comprehension. He then placed the handkerchief in his bosom with a reverent care, which was hardly exaggerated, bowed

155

very low, and turned to leave the room, as if unconscious of everything but his message.

His quick, assured movement took them by surprise; no one attempted to stop him, and the gendarmes in charge of the door looked inquiringly at the judge as Henri approached.

"Yes, let him go," said the judge, and the door was opened. But Léonore noticed with alarm that, at a sign from the dark man, one of the gendarmes slipped out also and followed him. But Henri was quick enough to notice this himself, and acted upon his instant resolution. He set off at a quick regular trot down the street in the direction which they had come that morning, repeating aloud as he ran, "Villeneuve! Villeneuve! Villeneuve!"

He had not gone in this way very long before he became aware that the man, who had at first followed him briskly, was falling behind. Evidently he did not see the fun of chasing an idiot boy out of the town under such a broiling sun, and his footsteps soon ceased altogether. Henri, on hearing this, gradually slackened his pace, and when he had got quite out of the town again, and felt certain that no one was in sight, he ventured to stop altogether, and flung himself for a few minutes on the grass beneath the hedge.

After making quite sure that he was not observed in any way, he drew out the handkerchief which Léonore had given him, expecting that at the last minute she would have managed to slip something into its folds. Nor was he mistaken; for he found a scrap of cambric, evidently torn off beforehand from some portion of her attire, on which, in faint red characters, as if they had been written with the point of a pin dipped in blood, he read these words:

> *Adieu, mon ami.* Forgive me, and leave at once. You can do nothing more for me; I am safe. Thank you forever. *Adieu.*

It took him some time to make this out, and he thought with a pang of what it must have cost her to write it. He was still reading it over, when he heard footsteps on the road, and instinctively he sprung over a low wall, and concealed himself till the traveller had passed. Hiding there, he began to consider seriously what to do next. To find Guillaume and Marie, and consult them. Good; but how? Clearly they would not be anywhere on this side of the town; probably they were trying to discover his whereabouts within it. He knew it would be madness for him to venture back into the streets again; there were too many to recognize him.

At this moment he heard fresh footsteps on the road, coming this time toward the town instead of from it. He cowered still lower behind the wall, and listened as they drew near. Hark! There was one whistling. It was the tune of the Soldiers of the Cross.

Forgetting all prudence in the instant conviction, Henri sprung out into the road again, and the next instant was clasped in Marie's arms. A torrent of eager questions followed, and somewhat incoherent rapture, on the part of all three. Then recollecting the danger he still ran, Henri drew them aside from the road, and they made their way to a small thicket, lying at a little distance within the field, where Henri narrated his adventures.

He learned, in return, that Guillaume and Marie had been hanging about the prison at Porte St. Marie almost the whole of last night, without being able to discover any news, and it was only this morning that they accidentally discovered that both the prisoners had been taken yesterday to Marmande for judgment. They had set out at once, intending to discover them by the same means, and it was only just, on nearing the town that Guillaume began to whistle the tune which had produced Henri before them, as it were by magic.

They agreed that Henri should remain concealed where he was, and Marie with him, while Guillaume should go cautiously into the town, buy some food — of which they all stood in need — and, if possible, learn the whereabouts of the convent in which Léonore was confined. Guillaume accordingly departed, and Henri and Marie spent the time of his absence in devising impossible means of rescuing Léonore, but could not help a conviction that, after all, they were impracticable.

It was late in the afternoon when Guillaume came back, and he brought but little encouragement. He had found out where the convent was, but could not find any way of approach to it, as it was shut in on all sides with high walls in the midst of the town. His idea was that they should all sleep, if possible, for the next two or three hours, and then Henri and Marie should make a circuit of the town, and wait for him on the other side, while he went through by the convent again, and made another attempt to communicate with Léonore under cover of the night. Then he would join them in the morning, and they would be able to get away before there was any fresh stir.

"And leave Léonore!" exclaimed Marie.

Guillaume was silent.

"What can we do?" said Henri, in a low tone, full of pain. "There seems no chance of rescuing her again, and if we delay, we run the risk of being taken ourselves, without being able to help or even to see her."

"Oh," cried Marie, with a gesture of despair, "shall we ever be sure of each other again? After all the rest — first Louis, and now Léonore."

Henri hid his face. Guillaume, after a few minutes' silence, whistled slowly the chorus of the Soldiers de St. Croix.

"You must whistle that tonight, Guillaume," said Marie, looking up, and trying to speak calmly again. "And now you and Henri must lie down and go to sleep. I could not sleep just now, if I were to try; so I will wake you by-and-by, lest we should not have time."

After a little persuasion the boys consented to do so, and Marie agreed to wake them after it had been quite dark about an hour. They fell asleep almost directly, and Marie sat between them, with her back against a tree, watching the sunlight slant more and more between the branches, till at length it seemed to strike upward instead of down. Then it sunk altogether, and a pale red hush spread itself over the sky, and faded away. It grew dusk, and Marie wondered how long they had been sitting there. She began to feel very drowsy, and had to pinch herself to keep awake. She looked at the boys — there was still light enough to see their faces — they were sleeping soundly. She was struck by the little difference that they showed, now that they were both asleep. Guillaume was nearly as tall as Henri, and their features were very similar, but in expression and colouring they differed entirely. Henri's frank, open face was as like his father's as his brown hair and eyes. In Guillaume's dreamy reserve and pale, almost sallow complexion, he was like no one else in the family, except, perhaps, Father Gabriel. His hair was as black as Marie's, but he had a magnificent pair of gray eyes under their heavy fringe of black eyelashes. Marie thought of her little Louis, so different from these two, and lately so like Aurèle. She wondered what he was doing now, and pulled herself up with a start, just as she was falling asleep again.

It was quite dark now, and Marie began to wonder how she should know when an hour had passed. In fact, she was so afraid of letting them oversleep themselves, and the time seemed so long, that she waked them in reality scarcely half an hour afterwards; but they were quite ready for the night's work.

Henri and Marie set off to walk round the town, and Guillaume crossed the field into the highroad by himself. There was none about, and very little stir even in the town when he approached it; some of the houses had already shut up for the night, but in the principal street there was a good deal going on, as, in fact, it was scarcely ten o'clock by the time Guillaume reached the town. He soon found that it was too early to do much near the convent, so he withdrew into the quieter streets, and sat down by the river-side for some time, watching the moon rise over the houses.

At length he became aware that everything had grown still around him, and that the whole town had gone to sleep. He rose from his seat, and walked away toward the convent, which was at no great distance. Its high dark walls and general outline reminded him very much of the one from which they had taken Léonore, but this one was surrounded by an outer wall about twenty feet high, and the convent itself stood some way back within it. A narrow, dark alley led round the wall from the street to the back of the convent.

Guillaume went down this and came out in a quiet open space covered with short grass, evidently the drying-ground of the convent. The moonlight now made everything clearly visible, and he thought perhaps it might be possible to climb up on the wall by means of one of the buttresses with which it was strengthened here and there. With great difficulty and many falls he succeeded at last in getting sufficiently high to look over the wall. On the other side also it went down straight for twenty feet to a stony gravel path. There were no trees anywhere along the whole line of wall by which he might have obtained a hold. The convent here advanced nearer to the wall than in front, and a long line of windows fronted him not thirty feet from where he clung. There was no sign of life about the place; all was dark and silent. After a minute or two Guillaume began softly to whistle the Soldiers de St. Croix, and paused in the middle.

There was no answer, except that he fancied something stirred in one of the rooms just opposite, and after waiting some time, and feeling that he could not hold on much longer, he began again.

This time a window opposite to him was slowly and noiselessly opened, and a white figure showed itself for an instant. Guillaume held his breath and bent his head out of sight for a moment, to consider whether he was safe or not. As he stooped he heard the tune continued, very faintly but still a continuation and not an echo.

He looked up, and there, leaning out into the moonlight, he saw Léonore. She was kneeling on the sill, with her long gleaming hair falling all around her, and even at that distance Guillaume could see how her eyes shone. They did not dare to speak to each other; they were not near enough for that. But she kissed her hand to him once, and then waved to him to go away. Guillaume answered by a gesture as if to leap down inside the wall, but her horrified signs reminded him the next moment of the extreme folly and uselessness of such a proceeding. She still urgently signed to him to go, and he felt that his feet were slipping. He held up something, and made signs that he wanted to throw it in: it was only a fold of paper on which they had written a farewell letter that afternoon, earnestly hoping against

160

hope that they might not need to send it, and contained a little gold cross, which she would know for Marie's, and two locks of short hair cut from the boys' heads.

Léonore moved aside a moment from the narrow window, and he threw it straight into the little cell; then she leant out again for a moment. And so he saw her for the last time, with the light on her tawny hair and her softened yearning face. Then his feet slipped again, and he half fell, half slipped to the ground, and so went sorrowfully away to join his brother and sister on their weary journey again.

XVIII

FISH-BARRELS

Bordeaux at last! A wild September evening drawing in rapidly; a fresh smell of the sea blowing up the broad river; a general air of business and prosperity; and three children standing silently, a little aside from the crowd, in one of the largest of the docks.

They had slept the previous night at a little village only a mile or two from the town, and had arrived at Bordeaux early, in order that they might have the whole day before them to gain intelligence about a ship. They had been somewhat dismayed on finding how very little money they had left, but still hoped to find it enough to pay their passage to Amsterdam. They had grown much more cautious since the arrest at Marmande, and therefore did not like to make many direct inquiries for what they wanted, and as they scarcely knew how to set about gaining the information they wanted, they had lingered about the docks all day without coming to any definite arrangement. They knew that there was now a strict law forbidding all Protestants to leave the country under pain of death, and were disinclined to put themselves into the power of a stranger, as to a certain extent they must do if they went openly to engage a passage. The circumstance of three children embarking alone was in those times sufficient in itself to cause suspicion.

Deep in thought, they did not notice that they had even now been for the last ten minutes the objects of a close scrutiny, until a young man, about twenty years of age, evidently a gentleman, approached Henri and said, in good French, but with a slight foreign accent,

"Monsieur has been waiting some time; can I have the pleasure of being of any service to him?"

He took off his hat with a graceful recognition of Marie's presence as he spoke, and stood before them — a tall, well-made young fellow, with fair hair, bright blue eyes, and a very un-French expression of countenance. Seeing that Henri hesitated, he smiled, and said, "Monsieur is a stranger in Bordeaux, is he not?"

"Yes; we have only arrived this morning," answered Henri slowly, still uncertain as to how far they might trust this new friend.

"Monsieur must then allow me to introduce myself. I am Harold van Eyck, nephew by marriage to Monsieur d'Ivray, who is master of these docks."

Marie looked up with a sudden light of relief. Few of the Protestant refugees had not heard by this time of Monsieur d'Ivray and his kindness to the Reformed. Men said that he was of the religion in heart, and only called himself Roman Catholic for the better service of the cause.

Harold van Eyck saw her glance, and remarked to Henri, "Mademoiselle has heard, I see, of my uncle's name. I have noticed that Monsieur has been trying to get information of some kind all day. Perhaps, if Monsieur would trust me, I might be able to help him."

"We were looking for a vessel ready to sail without delay for Amsterdam," said Henri, allowing his natural frank smile to appear.

The young man bowed. "Exactly," he replied; "I think we have one or two starting almost immediately. But it is becoming cold here for Mademoiselle your sister. May I suggest that you should accompany me to visit my uncle, who will be able to furnish you with all particulars?"

Henri looked at his sister. "Will you go Marie?" he asked in a tone intended for her alone.

"Yes," said Marie, without any hesitation. "We know Monsieur d'Ivray; he is a man to be trusted."

Henri therefore accepted the proposal as courteously as it had been made, and they followed their new friend out of the dockyard.

Marie noticed that he seemed to be known to every one they met, and that almost every one touched his cap in token of respect. They went a little way down the principal street, and stopped at the door of a large handsome house. An old man opened the door to them, and at a few words from their conductor, in a language which the children did not think was either English or German, ushered them into a small, neatly-furnished room, and left them there alone.

They looked at each other with a curious sense of mingled relief and perplexity. Were they at an end of their troubles, or only in a fresh one? They had not time to exchange many words about it before Harold returned, and with him a tall elderly Frenchman with a keen, grave, though at the same time a kindly face. He announced himself as Monsieur d'Ivray, and inquired their business, somewhat formally.

"We are ashamed thus to intrude upon you," began Henri frankly; "but Monsieur your nephew assured us that you would be good enough to give information as to the best way of taking our passage for Amsterdam."

"In a Roman Catholic or a Protestant ship?" asked Monsieur d'Ivray gravely. "Monsieur need not be afraid to answer me."

"In a Protestant ship, then," answered Henri. "One does not fear to inform Monsieur d'Ivray that we are of the Reformed religion."

"So we supposed," said Harold, who had not before spoken, and with the bright smile which had irresistibly inspired them with confidence. "It is all right, I think, mine uncle."

"You know that there is now a law forbidding all Protestants to leave the country," said Monsieur d'Ivray.

"We have heard so, Monsieur," replied Henri sadly. "But we are determined to do so if possible. If we cannot manage it from Bordeaux, we shall try somewhere else."

"The right spirit," answered Monsieur d'Ivray, with a smile and a look of interest. "I would not be too curious, my young Monsieur, but I seem to find a likeness in that face to someone whom I used to know."

"O Monsieur, can you have known our father?" exclaimed Marie eagerly; while Henri, at the same time, answered, "Our father was Louis de St. Croix of St. Croix, and of St. Louis-de-Linard in the Cévennes."

"Are you indeed the children of Monsieur de St. Croix?" said Monsieur d'Ivray, as he took Marie's hand, and looked earnestly into her beautiful eyes. "I did not know your father well, my dear young lady, but I did know him, and respected no man more. In him we have lost a wise and brave nobleman, as well as a true Christian."

The tears came into Marie's eyes, and the two boys came also nearer to this man who had known their father.

Harold van Eyck exclaimed impulsively, "It is all right then, is it not, mine uncle? We can at once explain to them the way of leaving Bordeaux."

"Certainly," said Monsieur d'Ivray, with far more readiness than before. "Are you afraid to be a little cramped and uncomfortable for a time, Mademoiselle?"

The three children looked at each other with a half smile. "We have spent two nights in an oven before now," said Henri in a low tone.

"That is a good preparation," said Harold, laughing, but checking himself when he saw the sad look on Marie's face. He rose from his seat and opened a small door, which looked as if it led to a cupboard, but which displayed instead a narrow dark passage, down which Monsieur d'Ivray proceeded to light them.

They came out into a small yard in the open air, in which there were standing several large barrels, such as were used for exporting fish. From this yard another door led into the outer and general yard, where they could see men busily at work in packing the barrels. Monsieur stooped down and held the light into one of the barrels, which was lying on its side. "I am afraid Mademoiselle will find it a little dark and musty," he said; "but it is the only way in which we can safely transport her on board ship."

"Must we all get in there?" said Marie, slightly dismayed at the prospect. "It will be worse than the oven."

"Oh, not all, Mademoiselle," exclaimed Harold "We can at least supply you with a barrel apiece, so that you will not be suffocated."

165

"It is *very* kind of you," said Marie, turning to Monsieur d'Ivray with tears in her eyes. "We do not know how to thank you."

Also Guillaume and Henri endeavoured to express their gratitude for the unexpected boon thus conferred on them, and Henri asked how soon the vessel would start.

"One leaves, in command of my nephew there, tomorrow at daybreak," answered Monsieur d'Ivray. "If that is not too soon for you, I will engage that he will be proud and glad to render any service to the children of Monsieur de St. Croix."

Harold most warmly seconded the plan, and it was ultimately agreed to by all. Moreover, Monsieur d'Ivray insisted on their remaining as his guests for the night, and took them in to a magnificently furnished sitting-room, where his wife received them with the greatest ease and cordiality. She was well accustomed to entertaining Protestant fugitives by this time, for Monsieur d'Ivray made a regular practice of thus facilitating their escape from France.

For the first time for more than three weeks — it seemed rather three years, so much had happened in that short time — they lay down to rest in a luxuriously appointed bedroom, and Marie, as she bade Henri goodnight in the presence of their hostess, touched her long black hair — a little rough from the windy day — with a smile, and the slightest possible shrug of her French shoulders. However, she found a maid waiting for her when she got upstairs, and had to submit to a much more vigorous brushing than she had been used to for some time.

They were wakened very early in the morning, and came down to a substantial breakfast with only Monsieur d'Ivray and Harold, whose brightness and fun were so infectious that the children grew merrier than they had done for a long time. Madame d'Ivray sent an excuse by her husband — she could never make up her mind to begin the day so early.

The vessel was to start at twelve, and all the real cargo had, of course, been shipped before. This was a last load, containing two or three barrels of merchandise, in case the royal officers should insist on examination, and in the centre were the three which were to contain Marie, Henri, and Guillaume.

Immediately after breakfast they proceeded down the passage into the same yard that they had seen last night. Here a cart, upon which the barrels were already placed, was waiting, and two men with it, who were evidently accustomed to the work, and touched their hats with a sympathetic smile at the young fugitives. It was still dusk, and the whole thing seemed very strange and unreal.

"Shall I go first?" asked Henri, seeing that his sister hesitated.

Marie looked up at him with a smile of relief, and bidding goodbye to Monsieur d'Ivray, he sprung at once upon the cart, and dived down to the bottom of his barrel, whence his voice was heard assuring them that it was rather a jolly place than otherwise.

"Ah! but how now?" laughed Harold, clapping the top on, which had one or two small rough holes in it for breathing.

Henri answered by a faint and stifled crow; after which Guillaume climbed into the next, and waited half-out to hold out his hand to Marie.

"I will help Mademoiselle in," said Harold, extinguishing the boy with the lid, and leaving it to be fastened while he went to assist Marie.

Marie turned to Monsieur d'Ivray with a sweet, grateful look in her dark eyes, which thanked him sufficiently, even had it not been for the few faltering words which were all she could say. "And oh, Monsieur!" she said, turning to the young Dutch baron, "shall we be able to come out of hiding before we are out of sight of France?"

"I will take care that it shall be so, Mademoiselle," answered the young man with respectful sympathy.

Then Marie climbed up into the cart, and lowered herself into the great musty barrel. It was cold and uncomfortable, certainly, especially when the lid was shut down on her, and the strange jolting ride began.

It seemed a long way to the docks, and there was no change until they had passed through the gates, when there was a sudden stoppage, and even through the wood she could hear rough voices in hot altercation with their conductors. Then followed a few moments of dreadful suspense and sundry blows upon the barrels, and then the cart went on again for about a quarter of a mile further. Then they stopped again, and listening intently, Marie guessed that they had arrived at the vessel. She heard the barrels taken off one after another, and wondered if the boys had gone first. Then she felt her own barrel laid hold of, and prepared herself for a shock; but was lifted off with very little movement, and carried, as she supposed, on to the vessel. Then there was a confusion of noises, out of which she could not distinguish anything, and she began to feel, though very slightly, the motion of the vessel. She was thankful to find that it did not upset her in the least, and wondered how the boys were getting on. The atmosphere of the barrel began to feel unpleasantly close and stuffy, and her thoughts, in spite of herself, went back to those terrible nights in the oven at St. Louis-de-Linard. Her head began to feel very dizzy and at length she fell into a kind of uneasy sleep, from which she was awakened by a vigorous knocking, and became aware that her prison was being opened.

In a few minutes the lid was removed, and pulling herself up, she was helped out by Henri; Harold van Eyck and the two men whom they had seen in the yard were also there.

"Where is Guillaume?" she asked.

"In this barrel," said Henri, pointing to the next, on which the two men were already hard at work.

Marie looked round her, but had only obtained a confused view of the hold of a ship, before an exclamation from Henri made her turn round again. The lid of Guillaume's barrel was off, but he did not appear.

"Guillaume! Guillaume!" cried Henri, bending over the edge. "Monsieur, the light!" He caught the light from the young baron's hand without ceremony, and held it within the barrel. Guillaume lay in a strange heap at the bottom, with his face downwards.

"Guillaume! Guillaume!" cried Henri again springing down beside him, while Marie, white, and with a terrible alarm, took the lamp from him.

"Give him out to me," said a strong, tender voice beside her, and Harold van Eyck leaned over the edge with outstretched arms.

With some difficulty Henri managed to raise his brother sufficiently for Harold to reach him. Then he was speedily lifted out, seemingly quite lifeless, with his head hanging back and his face deadly pale.

"We must get him into the air immediately," said Harold, striding on at once, closely followed by Marie and Henri.

A rush of fresh salt air met them as they emerged from the ladder, and laid Guillaume on a bench by the bulwark. One of the sailors went off for some brandy, and they tried to make him swallow a little; but it ran out again — there was no sign of life.

He was still supported by Harold, and Marie knelt by his side trying to get down some of the brandy, while Henri chafed his hands. The two men, who had now followed them up from the hold, stood silently behind in an awkward sympathy.

Some minutes must have passed in this way, and Marie, growing sick at heart with dumb apprehension, had ceased from her hopeless task, when there was a slight flutter of the eyelids, a faint gasp and the next moment — a moment Marie never forgot — the great, beautiful eyes opened quietly and the pale lips moved in speech. "De St. Croix — unto death!" he murmured. Then, as his consciousness came back, he tried to raise himself with an exclamation, but fell back fainting again. Marie eagerly administered the brandy, and this time it did not fail. He swallowed some of it, and a faint colour came back to his cheek. In a few moments he was able to sit up again and answer their questions. He said he was not conscious of having fainted, and recollected the first stoppage in the dock; but supposed the confinement had stifled him soon after, as he could remember nothing more. He was very anxious to get to the other side of the vessel to see the shore, which the other two had forgotten all about.

Harold found them very comfortable places on the other side, and left them alone together to watch the retreating shores of their native land. They were already out of sight of Bordeaux, and the green slopes along the coast looked very bright and peaceful in the noonday sun.

The three children sat hand in hand gazing, with feelings too deep for speech, at poor, distracted, yet "fair" France. Almost all day they sat there gazing, and when they came back again from a brief survey of their berths, which Harold had persuaded them to make, the sun was stooping down toward the sea, and the land was flushed with gold.

The ship seemed to be sailing on toward the light, and a low black cloud came up above the golden lighted land.

"New light, new life, and new friends!" murmured Henri as they turned westward, and the setting sun shone upon their faces.

"But we carry the old in our hearts, and are De St. Croix through it all!" whispered Marie, slipping her hand in his.

XIX

A Safe Home in a New Land

"Harold, Harold, what is that long white line of coast?"

"That, Henri? These are the white cliffs of the greatest country in the world."

"That is France!" put in Guillaume, quickly and defiantly.

Harold van Eyck laughed good-humouredly, and leaning his arms on the bulwark, gazed without answering at the white cliff rising out of the bright silvery mist which seemed to lie between them and the distant sea

"Are you so proud of England, Harold?" asked Marie thoughtfully. "I always thought one could never love any country so well as one's own."

"Doubtless, Mademoiselle," answered Harold, turning round at once; "but when one has two countries?"

"Are you English yourself, then?" exclaimed Marie in astonishment. "I thought you belonged to Amsterdam."

"My father is a Hollander, but my mother was English, and she was the best woman that ever walked the earth."

"I didn't know that," said Henri with interest. "What was your mother's name?"

"Lady Marion Maynard, daughter of an English earl," said Harold, with a loving accent on his mother's name. "It is after her father that I was christened Harold."

"I never heard the name before, but I like it very much," said Marie simply.

"Thank you, Mademoiselle," answered Harold with a bow. He and the young people had become great friends by this time, and he had exchanged Christian names with the boys, who admired him immensely. On the whole they had had a very pleasant voyage, and Harold van Eyck had taken care that they should not find it dull. Sometimes, he said, the barrels had been more full of fugitives than of fish, and once, in a time of stricter persecution a few months ago, he had taken as many as fifty passengers at one time; but on this occasion Marie and her brothers were the only people on board besides the crew.

Sometimes they talked of Amsterdam, and he did his best to describe the city and the customs of the Dutch, where they differed from the French. Henri brought out the letter which his father had left for them, and asked if he knew the name. Yes; he had met the lady once or twice, and believed she was charming, but did not know her so well as he now hoped to do. He believed she was French; perhaps she was a relation of theirs. But this Marie did not know — she believed not.

"We ought to get into port tomorrow," said Harold, as he turned to look over the sea again.

"What time do you think it will be?" asked Henri.

"Well, if this wind holds on, we ought to be in the harbour early in the afternoon. You will be able to reach Madame van der Hulst before the evening."

"Oh dear," sighed Marie, "I am so tired of new places and new people."

"Thank you, Mademoiselle," answered Harold in an odd, half-offended tone.

Marie turned quickly. "Harold, you could not think I meant you. We look on you quite as an old friend now; but that is just what I mean. One is no sooner at home, and happy, than one has to uproot oneself again, and begin once more at the beginning."

"Unfortunately, Mademoiselle, old friends must first be new, and it is not for me to regret your necessity for making new friends."

"I do not feel as if Amsterdam were to be our permanent home," said Henri. "I agree with you so far, Harold, that if one cannot be French, it is best to be English. And if I may never own St. Croix again, in France, I will plant a new one, not in Holland, but in England."

"And you, too, Mademoiselle, is your heart fixed on England?" asked Harold of Marie.

Marie's eyes met those of her brother with a smile. "Where Henri goes I will go, and his country shall be mine," she answered.

Harold turned away again rather abruptly, and walked off to another part of the vessel. The three children drew nearer to each other, and began to talk of their arrival at Amsterdam.

It was not until past four o'clock that they actually found themselves in the harbour at Amsterdam. The crowd and bustle seemed strange and alarming to the new-comers, unused as they had been to anything beyond their country home.

Harold had been very much occupied in business for the last hour, but he now came up to them as they stood together on the deck, with their scanty bundle at their feet, uncertain how to proceed.

"I can spare half an hour just now, Mademoiselle, to see you safe on your way to Madame van der Hulst, if you are ready to go."

"Yes; we are quite ready," said Marie, rather mournfully, "except one thing . . . Henri!"

Henri blushed up to the eyes as he stepped aside to speak with Harold. "Monsieur d'Ivray said we were to settle with you," he began, hesitatingly; but Harold cut him short in a moment.

"Of course, Henri; it is all settled. You must not speak of anything further. Monsieur d'Ivray will be well satisfied, as I have been, to render any service to the children of Monsieur de St. Croix."

"You are too good," faltered Henri, as he held out his hand. "We owe you both a debt which we can never repay."

"I am repaid already," answered the young man warmly. "Come, *mon ami*; we must not keep Mademoiselle your sister waiting.

They descended into the boat, which lay ready, and pushed off. A few minutes brought them to the landing-place. And here they would have been assailed by a host of the creatures who frequent such places, but a few sharp words from Harold, whom they recognized, soon dispersed them, and, followed only by one of the boatmen, who carried the small bundle of things which they had brought from St. Louis-de-Linard, they made their way into one of the principal streets.

"Madame van der Hulst lives a little way out of the town," said Harold, as he stopped and sent the boatman for one of the unwieldy carriages then in use; an extravagance which Marie was going to protest against, but for a sign from Henri, who had not been able to tell her yet that he still had all the money they had when they left Bordeaux.

"How long does it take to drive there?" asked Marie, as the conveyance came lumbering up.

"Not more than half an hour," answered Harold. "You will be there soon after six o'clock, I hope. I wish I could have seen you safely to the door; but I fear I must not stay longer now."

He was assisting Marie into the carriage as he spoke, and turned to the boys, who were waiting to bid him farewell before they followed.

"It is not goodbye, you know," he said, with a warm grasp of Henri's hand, according to the English custom in which he had been brought up. "I shall be in Amsterdam for some time now, and you must let me come and see how you get on with Madame van der Hulst."

"Yes, do," answered all the three voices together, while Guillaume added, "You promised to show us about Amsterdam, you know, and we will have no one else — will we, Marie?"

"The strange land seems less strange already, now that we have one old friend in it," said Marie, smiling, as she held out her hand to him.

He bowed in answer, and then the carriage jolted forward, and they left Harold to go back to his work, while they went on to their unknown home.

They had often discussed the end of their journey before; but now that it seemed to have actually arrived they were all nervous and restless. They had not the least idea what connection there had been between this lady and their father, nor how she was likely to receive them. Henri, indeed, had an indistinct idea, that a cousin of his father, of whom he had been very fond, had married a Hollander, but could not remember ever having heard his name.

It began to grow dusk, for it was now the middle of October, and the days were no longer very warm. Marie shivered a little, which made Henri begin to look round in order to see if there was nothing she could put on, and it was then that they discovered a warm fur cloak which Harold had been carrying over his arm, and which he had put unperceived by them into the carriage.

"Just like Harold," commented Henri, as he proceeded to wrap it round his sister.

"Yes," said Marie, thoughtfully. "After all, Henri, it seems wrong to fear these strangers so much. One can see God is taking care of us; for how wonderfully kind every one has been all the way."

They had been passing through busy and tolerably well-lighted streets, but now all shops disappeared, and tall large houses stood back from the road in gardens of their own. At one of these the driver suddenly stopped, and getting down, announced that this was the house of Madame van der Hulst. It looked very grand and imposing, and the children felt more strange and shy than ever, as they got out and walked up the path to the house: there was no way that they could see of driving up to the door.

"If we had only been able to make ourselves look a little less like peasants," sighed Marie, as they knocked at the door.

It was promptly opened by an imposing manservant, and another, equally grand, was visible in the distance. Seeing three poorly-dressed children, he instantly, and with a most disgusted expression shut it again in their faces.

"Encouraging!" remarked Guillaume, with his lazy smile of amusement. Marie gave a little nervous laugh, and Henri, a sudden

175

flush of anger restoring all his confidence, gave another and far more peremptory knock at the door.

The man put out his head, and said something angrily in Dutch which they did not understand, but Henri, putting his foot so that the door should not shut again, drew out his letter, and remarked coolly, "Carry that at once to your mistress, and tell her that Mademoiselle de St. Croix of St. Croix, with her two brothers, wait upon her."

The man's face underwent a ludicrous change. Suspicion struggled with a natural instinct of respect to the well-sounding name as he opened the door, and, allowing them to enter, looked doubtfully at his colleague, as if to entreat him to keep guard over them while he went upon his errand.

There ensued a few moments of trying suspense during which Henri conducted himself with an air of lordly indifference, which evidently made an impression upon the servant. Suddenly one of the great doors leading into the hall was thrown open and a tall, graceful woman, holding their father's letter open in her hand, came forward, with a quick, anxious glance.

Her eye fell upon Marie, and without giving the children time to greet her, she sprung forward and embraced her, with a burst of tears.

"O my child! My child!" she cried. "Thanks be to God! But only you — only three left?"

She embraced the two boys also as she spoke, much to the edification of the returning manservant, and led them straight into a beautiful drawing-room, full of warmth and light, where a gentleman, evidently Mynheer van der Hulst, greeted them warmly. With her own hands she removed Marie's cloak and hat, scarcely giving her time to answer the many questions she asked about themselves and their journey. She drew Henri forward into the light.

"His very image!" she exclaimed. "O my children, you have never known me, and yet your father and I were like brother and sister together. He did right to send you to me. And yet, how dreadful it all is! And I have been hoping all this time that he was safe in England. You must be, Marie, my child — yes, I am right — you are the likeness of your mother."

"Chère Célestine," here interposed her husband, who spoke French perfectly, but with a much stronger accent than Harold van Eyck, "the poor children must be half famished; let us have supper at once, and they shall tell us all about it afterwards."

His suggestion was immediately carried out, and while the supper was in preparation, Madame van der Hulst took Marie up to her own room to divest her of some of her garments, and cried over her as she bathed her forehead with essences and waited upon her with her own hands. And when, for the first time since she left St. Croix, Marie felt her feet in white silk stockings and soft, well-fitting satin slippers, she began to think she had never known what luxury was till now.

After supper they had a long quiet talk that was not altogether sad, while they related to their friends the terrible history of the last six weeks. Madame van der Hulst wept freely, and her husband sat silently listening with a thoughtful countenance. Long afterwards they could remember every detail of that first evening in their new home. And when at night Marie lay down on a bed which was a combination of delicate linen, lace, satin, and eider-down, with the blessed thought that their long strange journey was safely finished and their charge fulfilled, a sweet motherly face bent over her once more, and a tender voice, with a ring in it so like her father's, murmured, "My poor little one, Louis' child, you have done well, and, please God, we will make your new life a happy one!"

XX

NEW YEAR'S EVE

It was the last night of the old year. Here and there the bells of an Amsterdam church were already ringing in the still, frosty air, but on the whole the great city waited silently, half in sleep, half with careless or solemn expectation, for the coming of the year 1687. Outside the city, in a large and beautifully-furnished room — which, except for the richly-curtained bed standing in an alcove at the side, might have been taken for a drawing-room — Marie, Henri, and Guillaume de St. Croix were sitting watching for it together, talking, as they waited, of the year that had gone by.

Of the three children, Marie was the most changed since that sunny July day in the plantation at St. Croix. Then she would have been taken for less than her real age; now she looked at least fifteen, and many of Madame van der Hulst's friends supposed her to be sixteen. Perhaps it was partly caused by the fact that her thick black hair no longer tumbled about below her waist, but was skilfully and wonderfully arranged every morning by a tire-woman, who was almost as proud of it as Henri had been. Something also was due to the more womanly dress. On this evening she was attired in rich crimson velvet and delicate lace. But the chief change was in the face itself — in the earnest lines of the rose-bud mouth, and the womanly thoughtfulness of her beautiful dark eyes.

She was leaning back in a low, cushioned chair — not so comfortable as we make them now — and Guillaume was lying on the rug at her feet, in just the same attitude as he had lain on the grass in the old days. Henri was standing by them, in one of the attitudes so curiously like his father's, with his arm on the back of Marie's chair.

They were now fairly settled in their new life, and the old one, though fondly remembered, seemed a long time away. Henri and Guillaume attended a military school in Amsterdam, and Marie was taking lessons in all the accomplishments which were considered desirable for a young lady in that day.

Louis was still at Montauban — so they supposed — but they had never been able to hear of him, and after many fruitless inquiries, Mynheer van der Hulst decided that they could only wait — the lad was in the best place for him during the next year or two, and after that one could see.

They had not made many friends of their own age, though they knew several French refugees among the families which they visited. Harold van Eyck had established a close intimacy with the whole family, and had been in Amsterdam ever since October. He had been spending that evening at their house, and had promised to come and wish them a happy New Year on the morrow. Mynheer van der Hulst and his wife, who had always been childless, retired to their own room at the usual hour, and the three young people had by common consent come to watch together in Marie's room.

There had been a long silence between them for some time, broken by Henri, who said, with a deep sigh, "Do you remember New Year's eve last year, Marie, how merry we were — it was the first time we were allowed to sit up — and how every one came into the great hall at half past eleven, and we stopped our games after a while, and sang the Soldiers de St. Croix, just before twelve o'clock struck?"

"We will sing it again tonight," said Guillaume, from the rug. "What time is it, Henri?"

"Nearly half past eleven," said Henri, glancing at the clock.

"I remember," said Marie, thoughtfully, "something that struck me at the time, though I forgot it afterwards. Papa was tossing Louis in the air, and laughing with us all, when suddenly Mamma looked up at him, and said, 'O Louis! Where shall we all be this time next year?' And his face grew suddenly grave, and he said — it was the tone that struck me — 'God knows, Marie; we are in His hands!' "

"The edict must have been published then, though we did not know it," remarked Henri, huskily. "How strange to think that it is only a year ago!"

"Oh," said Marie, putting her hand up almost with a cry, "I cannot bear to talk of it, Henri. Mamma, Papa, Aurèle, Louis, home, and country — all lost!"

"We have lost much, but they have gained much. And we have also gained much," said Henri, "though even one's gains seem dreadful when one thinks of their price. Yet, Harold — Léonore . . ."

"We gained Léonore only to lose her again," said Marie. "If we could only hear of her and Louis."

"God knows, Marie; we are in His hands!" repeated Henri, and there was another long silence.

"It is nearly twelve," said Henri, at length. "Let us open the window and listen for the bells."

It was not very cold, and there was a bright starlit sky overhead as they leaned out. Then as they waited their hands joined and they sang the Soldiers de St. Croix. Now and then the voices faltered — they had never sung it since they left France — but the hand-clasp never faltered, and the young voices grew strong and full in the chorus at the end:

> *Then lift your hearts up comrades, comrades,*
> *Lift your hearts up to the Lord;*
> *Lo! for each one of us His soldiers*
> *There's a crown of glory stored.*
> *Much shall it profit us, comrades, comrades,*
> *If, for life-long toil and loss,*
> *We hear Him say, "Well done, my Soldiers,*
> *My brave Soldiers of the Cross!"*

As they finished, the bell of a church close by began to toll. Standing together, with bent heads and clasped hands, they listened to the twelve slow strokes, and the whole city seemed to wake up and shake the air with pealing bells as they kissed and wished each other a happy New Year.

Favourite Historical Novels for Juvenile Readers

Struggle for Freedom Series by Piet Prins

David Engelsma in the *Standard Bearer*: This is reading for Reformed children, young people, and (if I am any indication) their parents. It is the story of 12-year-old Martin Meulenberg and his family during the Roman Catholic persecution of the Reformed Christians in the Netherlands about the year 1600. A peddlar, secretly distributing Reformed books from village to village, drops a copy of Guido de Brès' *True Christian Confession* — a booklet forbidden by the Roman Catholic authorities. An evil neighbor sees the book and informs . . .

Time: 1568 - 1572   Age: 10-99
Vol. 1 - *When The Morning Came* ISBN 0-921100-12-4   Can.$9.95 U.S.$8.90
Vol. 2 - *Dispelling the Tyranny* ISBN 0-921100-40-X   Can.$9.95 U.S.$8.90
Vol. 3 - *The Beggar's Victory* (2004?) ISBN 0-921100-53-1 Can.$9.95 U.S.$8.90

J. Sawyer in *Trowel & Sword*, wrote about *When the Morning Came*:

From this well-known and loved author comes the tale of everyday little people in Holland in the 16th century.

The Meulenberg family and Martin their son have embraced the Reformed faith. As a result they face the wrath of the Spanish inquisition and the Roman church. They must flee for their lives to Germany.

It is so nice to read this story of everyday Christians and their truly heroic efforts to remain true to the Reformation of the Gospel. In a day when Christians are routinely portrayed as mindless idiots and bigots, here is a book which will help shape your child's thinking in a positive way: namely, to be Reformed is a blessed and honourable calling, and that we too must be prepared to confess and, if need be, die for that precious faith.

Excellent reading!

Christine Luimes in *The Trumpet*, wrote about Dispelling the Tyranny:

How much is the Reformed Faith worth to you! To Martin Meulenberg and his father it was worth everything. Martin and his parents lived during the time when they and other Dutch Reformed Christians where under great oppression because of the Spanish Inquisition.

In the previous book, *WHEN THE MORNING CAME*, they had managed to escape the Netherlands and flee to Germany where there was a city of refuge for Dutch protestants. Here they were free from persecution, yet they loved their homeland and were not content to leave it under oppression. Under the leadership of Count Lodewyk, the brother of the Prince of Orange, a small "beggars" army was preparing to fight for the freedom of Holland.

Martin was only a boy but he, too, loved his homeland and the Reformed faith. He badly wanted to help, after all, he was growing up wasn't he! After some unexpected opportunities arose for him to show his courage and bravery, and contribute valuably to the cause of freedom, he was on his way with the others, to adventure and excitement!

Adventure and excitement he got, and plenty of it. Several times he was near death. His escapes were breathtaking proofs of God's watchful protection of him. He met wonderful people, some of whom became his fast friends.

The little "beggars" army had victories and defeats, but they were courageous despite the many difficulties, because the love of God and His Church burned in their hearts.

This book gives the reader an inside view of history and shows again and again how God gives strength and courage to those who ask Him.

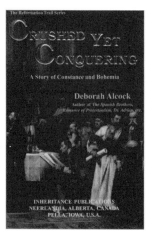

Crushed Yet Conquering
by Deborah Alcock

A gripping story filled with accurate historical facts about John Huss and the Hussite wars. **Hardly any historical novel can be more captivating and edifying than this book.** Even if Deborah Alcock was not the greatest of nineteenth century authors, certainly she is our most favourite.
— Roelof & Theresa Janssen

Time: 1414-1436	**Age: 11-99**
ISBN 1-894666-01-1	**Can.$19.95 U.S.$14.90**

The Spanish Brothers by **Deborah Alcock**

Christine Farenhorst in *Christian Renewal*: This historical novel, which is set in Spain a number of years after the Reformation, deals with the discovery of Reformed truth in that country . . . Two brothers, one a soldier and the other a student of theology, are the protagonists. Sons of a nobleman who disappeared when they were children, their search for him leads both to a confrontation with the Gospel. How they react, how their friends and relatives react to them, and what their struggles and thoughts are, form the main body of the book.

An excellent read, this book should be in every church and home library.

Time: 1550-1565	**Age: 14-99**
ISBN1-984666-02-x	**Can.$14.95 U.S.$12.90**

By Far Euphrates by **Deborah Alcock**
A Tale on Armenia in the 19th century

Alcock has provided sufficient graphics describing the atrocities committed against the Armenian Christians to make the reader emotionally moved by the intense suffering these Christians endured at the hands of Muslim Turks and Kurds. At the same time, the author herself has confessed to not wanting to provide full detail, which would take away from the focus on how those facing death did so with peace, being confident they would go to see their LORD, and so enjoy eternal peace. **As such it is not only an enjoyable novel, but also encouraging reading.** These Christians were determined to remain faithful to their God, regardless of the consequences.

Time: 1887-1895	**Age: 11-99**
ISBN 1-894666-00-3	**Can.$14.95 U.S.$12.90**

A Stranger in a Strange Land
by Leonora Scholte

John E. Marshall in *The Banner of Truth*: This is a delightful book. It tells the story of H.P. Scholte, a preacher in the Netherlands, who, being persecuted for his faith in his own country, emigrated to the U.S.A., and there established a settlement in Pella, Iowa, in the midst of the vast undeveloped prairie . . . It is a most heartwarming and instructive story.

Time: 1825-1880   **Age: 14-99**
   ISBN 0-921100-01-9   **Can.$7.95 U.S.$6.90**

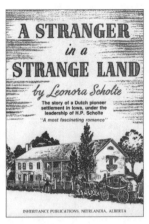

2nd Printing

Against the World
The Odyssey of Athanasius
by Henry W. Coray

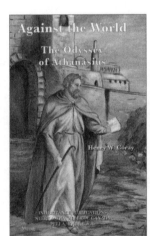

Muriel R. Lippencott in *The Christian Observer*: [it] . . . is a partially fictionalized profile of the life of Athanasius . . . who died in A.D. 373. Much of the historical content is from the writing of reliable historians. Some parts of the book, while the product of the author's imagination, set forth accurately the spirit and the temper of the times, including the proceedings and vigorous debates that took place in Alexandria and Nicea. . . This is the story that Rev. Coray so brilliantly tells.

Time: A.D. 331-373   **Age: 16-99**
ISBN 0-921100-35-3   **Can.$8.95 U.S.$7.90**

The Crown of Honour by L. Erkelens

Rachel Manesajian in *Chalcedon Report*: This book is about an illegitimate girl whose mother died when she was born, and no one knows who her father is. She grows up in an orphanage, and she goes through many hardships and is treated poorly because she is illegitimate. The few people she loves are taken away from her. Because of all her trials, she thinks God is against her, and so, in rebellion, she refuses to go to church or pray. However, the prayers of an old man who loves and prays for her are answered and she realizes . . . a wonderful story.

Fiction   **Age: 14-99**
ISBN 0-921100-14-0   **Can.$11.95 U.S.$10.90**

The Soldier of Virginia
A Novel on George
Washington by Marjorie Bowen

Originally published in 1912, this is a fictionalized biography on America's first President by one of the best authors of historical fiction.

Time: 1755-1775   Age: 14-99
ISBN 0-921100-99-X   Can.$14.95 U.S.$12.90

The Governor of England
by Marjorie Bowen
A Novel on Oliver Cromwell

An historical novel in which the whole story of Cromwell's dealings with Parliament and the King is played out. It is written with dignity and conviction, and with the author's characteristic power of grasping the essential details needed to supply colour and atmosphere for the reader of the standard histories.

Time: 1645-1660   Age: 14-99
ISBN 0-921100-58-2   Can.$17.95 U.S.$15.90

The Romance of Protestantism
by Deborah Alcock

The Romance of Protestantism addresses one of the most damaging and (historically) effective slanders against the Reformed faith, which is that it is cold and doctrinaire. What a delight to find a book which documents the true warmth of the Protestant soul. I recommend this book highly.
— Douglas Wilson, editor of *Credenda/Agenda*

Time: 1300-1700   Age: 12-99
ISBN 0-921100-88-4   Can.$ 11.95 U.S.$ 9.90

Coronation of Glory
by Deborah Meroff

The true story of seventeen-year-old Lady Jane Grey, Queen of England for nine days.

"Miss Meroff . . . has fictionalized the story of Lady Jane Grey in a thoroughly absorbing manner . . . she has succeeded in making me believe this is what really happened. I kept wanting to read on — the book is full of action and interest."

— Elisabeth Elliot

Time: 1537-1554　　　　　　　**Age: 14-99**
ISBN 0-921100-78-7　　**Can.$14.95 U.S.$12.90**

Captain My Captain by **Deborah Meroff**

Willy-Jane VanDyken in *The Trumpet*: This romantic novel is so filled with excitement and drama, it is difficult to put it down once one has begun it. Its pages reflect the struggle between choosing Satan's ways or God's ways. Mary's struggles with materialism, being a submissive wife, coping with the criticism of others, learning how to deal with sickness and death of loved ones, trusting in God and overcoming the fear of death forces the reader to reflect on his own struggles in life.

This story of Mary Ann Patten (remembered for being the first woman to take full command of a merchant sailing ship) is one that any teen or adult reader will enjoy. It will perhaps cause you to shed a few tears but it is bound to touch your heart and encourage you in your faith.

Time: 1837-1861　　　　　　　**Age: 14-99**
ISBN 0-921100-79-5　　**Can.$14.95 U.S.$12.90**

Journey Through the Night
by Anne De Vries

After the second world war, Anne De Vries, one of the most popular novelists in The Netherlands, was commissioned to capture in literary form the spirit and agony of those five harrowing years of Nazi occupation. The result was Journey Through the Night, a four volume bestseller that has gone through more than thirty printings in The Netherlands.

"An Old Testament Professor of mine who bought the books could not put them down — nor could I."

— Dr. Edwin H. Palmer

Time: 1940-1945　　　　　　　**Age: 10-99**
ISBN 1-984666-21-6　　**Can.$19.95 U.S.$14.90**

2nd Printing

Jessica's First Prayer & Jessica's Mother
by Hesba Stretton

Liz Buist in *Reformed Perspective*: There is much to be learned from this story. It is written primarily for children, but this book is worthwhile reading for adults as well . . . Highly recommended for young and older. *The Sword and Trowel* says (about *Jessica's First Prayer*): One of the most tender, touching, and withal gracious stories that we ever remember to have read. A dear little book for our children. We are not ashamed of having shed tears while reading it; in fact, should have been ten times more ashamed if we had not. The sweet portrait of the poor child Jessica is a study, and old Daniel is perfect in his own way.

Subject: Fiction   **Age: 9-99**
ISBN 0-921100-63-9   **Can.$8.95 U.S.$7.90**

2nd Printing

Probable Sons
by Amy Le Feuvre

The *Sword and Trowel* says: A lovely story that every-body — man, woman, boy, or girl — ought to read. The heroine is a charming child who, in a most winning way, applies to everyday life the Parable of the Prodigal Son, whom she mis-calls the Probable Son. It is scarcely possible to praise too highly this delightful volume.

Subject: Fiction   **Age: 8-99**
ISBN 0-921100-81-7   **Can.$6.95 U.S.$5.90**

Pilgrim Street
by Hesba Stretton

Little Phil desperately wants to see his brother Tom. He knows Tom isn't guilty. But Phil is afraid of the policeman. Who will help these street urchins?

Subject: Fiction   **Age: 9-99**
ISBN 0-921100-91-4   **Can.$8.95 U.S.$7.90**

Legend Led
by Amy Le Feuvre

Three children, orphaned at an early age and living with a governess, are suddenly sent for by an older step-brother who lives in the country. Steeped in Arthurian legends, Gypsy, the youngest of the three children, is convinced that the Holy Grail, or 'Holy Thing' as she calls it, is hidden somewhere on their brother's estate. When she does actually find the 'Holy Thing', it is not quite what she has expected. Reminiscent of W.G. VandeHulst, this book is sure to endear itself to parents as well as to young children. Most certainly recommended.

Subject: Fiction   **Age: 10-99**
ISBN 0-921100-82-5   **Can.\$8.95 U.S.\$7.90**

Little Meg's Children by Hesba Stretton

Christine Farenhorst in *Christian Renewal*: During the Victorian era a family, reduced to penury, lives in a squalid tenement awaiting their seafaring father's return. When the mother dies, the responsibility of caring for her two small brothers devolves to a very young girl. Having been initiated in the rudiments of Christianity through her mother's Bible reading, with child-like faith this little woman keeps her family going.

Reminiscent of W.G. VandeHulst, Stretton manages to pass on to her readers the importance of unquestioning faith in an omniscient God. Excellent reading.

Subject: Fiction   **Age: 9-99**
ISBN 0-921100-92-2   **Can.\$8.95 U.S.\$7.90**

Teddy's Button by Amy Le Feuvre

The Life of Faith says: Teddy's Button is by the author of *Probable Sons*, and it would be difficult to say which is the better.

Rev. Thomas Spurgeon says: A smile-provoking, tear-compelling, heart-inspiring book. I wish every mother would read it to her children.

The Christian says: A lively little story, telling of a lad whose military spirit found satisfaction in enlisting in Christ's army and fighting God's battles.

Subject: Fiction   **Age: 8-99**
ISBN 0-921100-83-3   **Can.\$7.95 U.S.\$6.90**

Hubert Ellerdale by W. Oak Rhind
A Tale of the Days of Wycliffe
Christine Farenhorst in *Christian Renewal*: Christians often tend to look on the Reformation as the pivotal turning point in history during which the Protestants took off the chains of Rome. This small work of fiction draws back the curtains of history a bit further than Luther's theses. Wycliffe was the morning star of the Reformation and his band of Lollards a band of faithful men who were persecuted because they spoke out against salvation by works. Hubert Ellerdale was such a man and his life (youth, marriage, and death), albeit fiction, is set parallel to Wycliffe's and Purvey's.

Rhind writes with pathos and the reader can readily identify with his lead characters. This novel deserves a well-dusted place in a home, school, or church library.

Time: 1380-1420	Age: 13-99
ISBN 0-921100-09-4	Can.$12.95 U.S.$10.90

Love in Times of Reformation
by William P. Balkenende

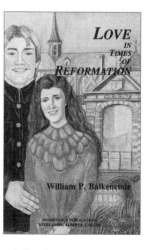

N.N. in *The Trumpet*: This historical novel plays in The Netherlands during the rise of the protestant Churches, under the persecution of Spain, in the latter half of the sixteenth century. Breaking with the Roman Catholic Church in favor of the new faith is for many an intense struggle. Anthony Tharret, the baker's apprentice, faces his choice before the R.C. Church's influenced Baker's Guild. His love for Jeanne la Solitude, the French Huguenot refugee, gives a fresh dimension to the story. Recommended! Especially for young people.

Time: 1560-1585	Age: 14-99
ISBN 0-921100-32-9	Can.$8.95 U.S.$7.90

The Heroes of Castle Bretten
by Margaret S. Comrie

"Now, young master, deliver to me that paper you carry!" commanded the man in a deep guttural voice. "It is against General Ruprecht's orders that dispatches go from the bridge to the castle save those sent with his knowledge."

Eleonore, Lady of Castle Bretten, has been alienated from her friends and allies by false rumours spread by her nephew, General Lucas von Ruprecht, Count of Zamosc. When Guido, a young Protestant, comes to live at the castle, he wins the love and trust of Lady Eleonore and Felix, the General's son. Guido and Felix uncover a plot to gain control of the castle. Together the heroes of Castle Bretten make the dangerous journey through the Gallows' Wood to get help.

Time: 1618-1648	Age: 11-99
ISBN 1-894666-65-8	Can.$14.95 U.S.$12.90

Driven into Exile
by Charlotte Maria Tucker

"His Majesty rejects my petition: I must either recant or quit France within twenty-one days."

"I hope — I doubt not — that Monsieur le Marquis will conform to the wishes of his Majesty," said the courtier blandly.

"In all that does not concern conscience," was the reply; "but my duty to God must come before even my duty to the King."

The Marquis la Force along with his wife and daughter are driven into exile to England. Making a life in a country the complete opposite of France is hard on the La Force family, especially when they hear that their son and brother Louis, still in France, is to be educated in the Roman Catholic religion. Meanwhile Adele la Force is having trouble coping with poverty and her step-mother. This is a story of the Lord strengthening this Huguenot family and keeping them together in spite of persecution and poverty.

Time: 1685-1695   Age: 13-99
ISBN 0-921100-66-3   Can.$9.95 U.S.$8.90

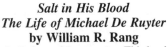

Done and Dared in Old France
by Deborah Alcock

Christine Farenhorst wrote in *Christian Renewal*: Ten-year-old Gaspard, accidentally separated from his parents, is raised by a group of outlaw salt runners who fear neither God nor man . . . Through the providence of God, Gaspard's heart turns to Him in faith and after a series of adventures is able to flee France to the safer Protestant shores of England. Fine and absorbing reading. Deborah Alcock has wonderful vocabulary, is a marvelous story-teller, and brings out the amazing hand of God's almighty power in every chapter. Highly recommended.

Time: 1685-1697   Age: 11-99
ISBN 1-894666-03-8   Can.$14.95 U.S.$12.90

Salt in His Blood
The Life of Michael De Ruyter
by William R. Rang

Liz Buist in *Reformed Perspective*: This book is a fictional account of the life of Michael de Ruyter, who as a schoolboy already preferred life at sea to being at school . . . This book is highly recommended as a novel way to acquiring knowledge of a segment of Dutch history, for avid young readers and adults alike.

Time: 1607-1676   Age: 10-99
ISBN 0-921100-59-0   Can.$10.95 U.S.$9.90

The William & Mary Trilogy by
Marjorie Bowen

The life of William III, Prince of Orange, Stadtholder of the United Netherlands, and King of England (with Queen Mary II) is one of the most fascinating in all of history. Both the author and the publisher of these books have been interested in this subject for many years. Although the stories as told in these books are partly fictional, all the main events are faithful to history.

F. Pronk wrote in *The Messenger* about Volume 1: The author is well-known for her well-researched fiction based on the lives of famous historical characters. The religious convictions of the main characters are portrayed with authenticity and integrity. This book is sure to enrich one's understanding of Protestant Holland and will hold the reader spell-bound.

D.J. Engelsma wrote in *The Standard Bearer* about Volume 1: This is great reading for all ages, high school and older. *I Will Maintain* is well written historical fiction with a solid, significant, moving historical base . . . No small part of the appeal and worth of the book is the lively account of the important history of one of the world's greatest nations, the Dutch. This history was bound up with the Reformed faith and had implications for the exercise of Protestantism throughout Europe. Christian high schools could profitably assign the book, indeed, the whole trilogy, for history or literature classes.

C. Farenhorst wrote in *Christian Renewal* about Volume 1: An excellent tool for assimilating historical knowledge without being pained in the process, *I Will Maintain* is a very good read. Take it along on your holidays. Its sequel *Defender of the Faith*, is much looked forward to.

Time: 1670-1702   **Age: 14-99**

Volume 1 - *I Will Maintain*
ISBN 0-921100-42-6   **Can.$17.95 U.S.$15.90**
Volume 2 - *Defender of the Faith*
ISBN 0-921100-43-4   **Can.$15.95 U.S.$13.90**
Volume 3 - *For God and the King*
ISBN 0-921100-44-2   **Can.$17.95 U.S.$15.90**